Jazzy gazed at Brooks in stunned silence. Had he asked her to do what she thought he'd asked her to do?

"I asked you to marry me. I know you think I'm absolutely crazy."

"No..." she started and didn't know quite how to finish or where to go from there.

"This isn't a joke, Jazzy. I'm not out of my mind. Really. But I need to solve this problem with my father. The only way he's going to let me in on the practice, the only way he's going to rest and stop wearing himself down, is if I'm really settled. I have to give him what he wants."

"I don't understand," she said very quietly.

"He wants me to have a wife, so I need a wife. The way we've worked together the past week, I just know you'd be perfect."

"So you really *do* want me to marry you?"

"It wouldn't be a real marriage."

When he said those words, she found herself amazingly disappointed. How stupid was that?

* * *

MONTANA MAVERICKS: RUST CREEK COWBOYS

Better saddle up. It's going to be a bumpy ride!

Dear Reader,

As a child, I often visited my cousins' farm. I was a teenager when I witnessed a foal being born. I'll never forget the way the veterinarian helped with the birth and watched over the mom and baby. I have always loved animals and adopted cats and dogs. Fortunately, we have had caring veterinarians to watch over them. These experiences were the basis for my hero Brooks's reverence for the profession and my heroine Jazzy's dream of managing a horse rescue ranch someday.

This romance between Brooks and Jazzy is a whirlwind one. Jazzy's feelings for Brooks escalated easily when she saw how much he cared for animals, as well as his dad. Brooks's feelings for her grew deeper and stronger because he saw her bonds with both the people around her and the animals he helped heal. These two were a perfect match from the start, even though they fought their attraction for as long as they could.

Brooks and Jazzy swept me along with them into their romance. I hope they do the same for you!

All my best,

Karen Rose Smith

Marrying
Dr. Maverick

—

Karen Rose Smith

Special thanks and acknowledgment to Karen Rose Smith for her contribution to the Montana Mavericks: Rust Creek Cowboys continuity.

Recycling programs
for this product may
not exist in your area.

ISBN-13: 978-0-373-65769-8

MARRYING DR. MAVERICK

Copyright © 2013 by Harlequin Books S.A.

HARLEQUIN®
™ www.Harlequin.com

Printed in U.S.A.

Books by Karen Rose Smith

Harlequin Special Edition

Silhouette Special Edition

Silhouette Books

Other titles by this author
available in ebook format.

KAREN ROSE SMITH

Award-winning and bestselling author Karen Rose Smith's plots are all about emotion. She began writing in her early teens, when she listened to music and created stories to accompany the songs. An only child, she spent a lot of time in her imagination and with books—Nancy Drew, Zane Grey, the Black Stallion and Anne of Green Gables. She dreamed of brothers and sisters and a big family such as the ones her mother and father came from. This is the root of her plotlines, which include small communities and family relationships as part of everyday living. Residing in Pennsylvania with her husband and three cats, she welcomes interaction with readers on Facebook, Twitter @karenrosesmith and through her website, www.karenrosesmith.com, where they can sign up for her newsletter.

To my family and friends who love animals as much as I do—my husband Steve, my son Ken, Suzanne, Sydney, Liz, Jane, Ryan, Heather, Abby, Sophie, Chris. Special thanks to my pet sitter, Barb, whose expertise allows me to leave home with a free heart.

Chapter One

Brooks Smith rapped firmly on the ranch-house door, scanning the all-too-familiar property in the dusk.

His dad didn't answer right away, and Brooks thought about going around back to the veterinary clinic, but then he heard footsteps and waited, bracing himself for this conversation.

After his father opened the door, he looked Brooks over, from the beard stubble that seemed to be ever present since the flood to his mud-covered boots. Tending to large animals required trekking through fields sometimes.

"You don't usually come calling on a Tuesday night. Run into a problem you need me for?"

Barrett Smith was a barrel-chested man with gray hair and ruddy cheeks. At six-two, Brooks topped him by a couple of inches. The elder Smith had put on another ten pounds over the past year, and Brooks realized he should have been concerned about that before today.

There was challenge in his dad's tone as there had been since they'd parted ways. But as a doctor with four years of practice under his belt, Brooks didn't ask for his dad's advice on animal care or frankly anything else these days.

"Can I come in?"

"Sure."

Brooks entered the living room where he'd played as a child. The Navajo rugs were worn now, the floor scuffed.

"I only have a few minutes," his father warned him. "I haven't fed the horses yet."

"I'll get straight to the point, then." Brooks swiped off his Stetson and ran his hand through his hair, knowing this conversation was going to get sticky. "I ran into Charlie Hartzell at the General Store."

His father avoided his gaze. "So?"

"He told me that when he stopped by over the weekend, you weren't doing too well."

"I don't know what he's talking about," his dad muttered, not meeting Brooks's eyes.

"He said you carried a pail of oats to the barn and you were looking winded and pale. You dropped the bucket and almost passed out."

"Anybody can have an accident. After I drank a little water, I was fine."

Not so true according to Charlie, Brooks thought. His dad's longtime friend had stayed another hour to make sure Barrett wasn't going to keel over.

"You're working too hard," Brooks insisted. "If you'd

let me take over the practice, you could retire, take care of the horses in the barn and help out as you want."

"Nothing has changed," Barrett said angrily. "You still show no sign of settling down."

This was an old argument, one that had started after Lynnette had broken their engagement right before Brooks had earned his degree in veterinary medicine from Colorado State. That long-ago night, his father had wanted to discuss it with him, but with Brooks's pride stinging, he'd asked his dad to drop it. Barrett hadn't. Frustrated, his father had blown his top, which wasn't unusual. What *was* unusual was his warning and threat—he'd never retire and turn his practice over to Brooks until his son found a woman who would stick by him and build a house on the land his grandmother had left him.

Sure enough…

"Your grandmama's land is still sitting there with no signs of a foundation," his dad went on. "She wanted you to have roots, too. That's why she left it to you. Until you get married and at least *think* about having kids, I can handle my own practice just fine. And you should butt out."

He could rise to the bait. He could argue with his father as he'd done before. But he didn't want his dad's blood pressure to go any higher so he stuck to being reasonable. "You can issue an ultimatum if you want, but this isn't about me. It's about you. You can't keep working the hours you've been working since the flood. You're probably not eating properly, grabbing donuts at Daisy's and potato chips at the General Store."

"Are you keeping track of what I buy where?"

"Of course not. I'm worried about you."

"Well, don't be. Worry about yourself. Worry about the life you don't have."

"I have a life, Dad. I'm living it *my* way."

"Yeah, well, twenty years from now you just tell me how that went. I'm going out back. You can see yourself out."

As his father turned to leave, Brooks knew this conversation had been useless. He knew he probably shouldn't even have come. He had to find a way to make his father wake up to the reality of his deteriorating health. He would…one way or another.

Jasmine Cates—"Jazzy" to her friends and family— stood outside the Ace in the Hole, Rust Creek Falls' lone bar, staring up at the wood-burned sign. She glanced around at the almost deserted street, hoping she'd catch sight of her friend Cecilia, who was tied up at a community meeting. They were supposed to meet here.

On the north side of town, the Ace in the Hole hadn't been touched by the devastating July flood, but Jazzy didn't know if she felt comfortable walking into the place alone. It was a rough and rowdy cowboy hangout, a place single guys gathered to relax. But when they relaxed, all hell could break loose. She'd heard about occasional rumbles and bar fights here.

Feeling as if she'd scrubbed herself raw from her shower at Strickland's Boarding House, attempting to wash off the mud from a disastrous date, she passed the old-fashioned hitching post out front and stared up at the oversize playing card—an ace of hearts—that blinked in red neon over the door. After she climbed two rough-hewn wooden steps, Jazzy opened the old screen door with its rusty hinges and let it slap behind her. A country tune poured from a jukebox. Booths lined the outer walls while wooden tables with ladder-back chairs were scattered across the plank flooring around a small dance floor. Jazzy glimpsed pool tables in the far back. Old West photos as well as those from local ranches hung on the walls. A wooden bar was situated on the right side of the establishment crowded with about a dozen bar stools, and a mirrored wall reflected the rows of glass bottles.

Cowboys and ranch hands filled the tables, and a few gave her glances that said they might be interested in talking…or more. Jazzy quickly glanced toward the bar. There was one bar stool open and it was next to—

Wasn't that Dr. Brooks Smith? She hadn't officially met him, but in her volunteer work, helping ranch owners clean up, paint and repair, she'd caught sight of him now and then as he tended to their animals. She'd liked the way he'd handled a horse that'd been injured. He'd been respectful of the animal and downright kind.

Decision made, she crossed to the bar and settled on the stool beside him. Brooks had that sexy, scruffy look tonight. He was tall and lean and broad-shouldered. Usually he wore a smile for anyone he came in contact with, but now his expression was granitelike, and his hands were balled into fists. It didn't even look like he'd touched his beer.

As if sensing her regard, and maybe her curiosity, he turned toward her. Their gazes met and there was intensity in his brown eyes that told her he'd been thinking about something very serious. His gaze swept over her blond hair, snap-button blouse and jeans, and that intensity shifted into male appreciation.

"You might need a bodyguard tonight," he drawled. "You're the only woman in the place."

He could be *her* bodyguard anytime. She quickly banished that thought. Hadn't she heard somewhere that he didn't date much? Love gone wrong in his romantic history?

"I'm meeting a friend." She stuck out her hand. "You're Brooks Smith. I'm Jazzy Cates. I've seen you around the ranches."

He studied her again. "You're one of the volunteers from Thunder Canyon."

"I am," she said with a smile, glad he'd recognized her.

When he took her hand to shake it, she felt tingles up her arm. That couldn't be, could it? She'd almost been engaged to a man and hadn't felt tingles like *that*. Brooks's grip was strong and firm, his hand warm, and when he took it away, she felt…odd.

"Everyone in town appreciates the help," he said.

"Rust Creek Falls is a tight-knit community. I heard stories about what happened after the flood. Everyone shared what was in their freezers so no one would go hungry."

Brooks nodded. "The community spirit was stoked by Collin Traub and the way he pulled everyone together."

"I heard about his proposal to Willa Christensen on Main Street but I didn't see it myself."

Brooks's eyes darkened at her mention of a proposal, and she wondered why.

"He and Willa seem happy" was all Brooks said.

So the man didn't gossip. She liked that. She liked a

lot about him. Compared to the cowboy she'd been out with earlier tonight—

A high-energy country tune played on the jukebox and snagged their attention for a moment. Jazzy asked, "Do you come here often?"

"Living and mostly working in Kalispell, I don't usually have the time. But I'll meet a friend here now and then."

Kalispell was about twenty miles away, the go-to town for everything anyone in Rust Creek Falls needed and couldn't find in their small town. "So you have a practice in Kalispell?"

"I work with a group practice there. We were called in to help here because my dad couldn't handle it all."

She'd heard Brooks's father had a practice in Rust Creek Falls and had assumed father and son worked together. Her curiosity was aroused. She certainly knew about family complications. "I guess you're not needed here as much now since the town's getting back on its feet."

"Not as much. But there are still animals recovering from injuries during the flood and afterward. How about you? Are you still cleaning out mud from homes that had water damage?"

"Yep, but I'm working at the elementary school, too."

"That's right, I remember now. You came with Dean Pritchett's group."

"Dean's been a friend of our family for years. He was one of the first to volunteer to help."

"How long can you be away from Thunder Canyon?"

"I'm not sure." Because Brooks *was* a stranger, she found herself saying what she couldn't to those closest to her. "My job was…static. I need a business degree to get a promotion and I've been saving for that. I came here to help, but I also came to escape my family. And…I needed a change."

"I can understand that," Brooks said with a nod. "But surely they miss you back home, and a woman like you—"

"A woman like me?"

"I'd think you'd have someone special back there."

She thought about Griff Wellington and the proposal he'd wanted to make and the proposal she'd avoided by breaking off their relationship. Her family had tried to convince her she should marry him, but something inside her had told her she'd known better. Griff had been hurt and she hated that. But she couldn't tie them both to a relationship she'd known wasn't right.

Maybe it was Brooks's easy way; maybe it was the interest in his eyes; maybe it was the way he listened, but she admitted, "No one special. In fact, I had a date tonight before I ended up here."

"Something about that doesn't sound right. If you had a date, why isn't he here with you?"

"He's a calf roper."

Brooks leaned a little closer to hear her above the music. His shoulder brushed hers and she felt heat other places besides there. "What does that have to do with your date?"

"That *was* the date."

Brooks pushed his Stetson higher on his head with his forefinger. *"What?"*

"Calf-roping. He thought it would be fun if he showed me how he did it. That would have been fine, but then he wanted *me* to do it. Yes, I ride. Yes, I love horses. But I'd never calf-roped before and so I tried it.

There was mud all over the place and I slipped and fell and I was covered with mud from head to toe."

Brooks was laughing by then, a deep, hearty laugh that seemed to echo through her. She liked the fact she could make him laugh. Genially, she bumped his arm. "It wasn't so funny when it was happening."

He gave her a crooked smile that said he was a little bit sorry he laughed, but not much. "Whatever gave him the impression you'd like to try that out?"

"I have no clue, except I did tell him I like horses. I did try to be interested in what he did, and I asked him questions about it."

"This was a first date?" Brooks guessed.

"It was the *last* date," Jazzy responded.

"Not the last date *ever*."

She sighed. "Probably not."

Was he thinking of asking her out? Or were they just flirting? With that twinkle in his eyes, she imagined he could flirt with the best of them if he really wanted to.

"So you came here to meet a friend and hash out everything that's happened," he concluded.

"My gosh, a guy who understands women!"

He laughed again. "No, not so well."

She wondered what *that* meant. "When I'm at home, sometimes I talk it all out with my sisters."

"How many do you have?"

"I have four sisters, a brother and parents who think they know what's best for me."

"You're lucky," Brooks said.

"Lucky?"

"Yep. I'm the only one. And I lost my mom a long time ago."

"I'm sorry."

He shrugged. "Water under the bridge."

But something in his tone said that it wasn't, so she asked, "Are you close to your dad?"

"He's the reason I stopped in here tonight."

"To meet him?"

"Nope." He hesitated, then added, "We had another argument."

"Another?"

Brooks paused again before saying, "My dad's not taking care of himself, and I can't give him what he wants most."

In her family, Jazzy usually said what she thought, and most of the time, no one heard her. But now she asked, "And what's that?"

"He wants me to marry, and I'll never do that."

Whoa! She wanted to ask that all-important question—why?—but they'd just officially met and she knew better than to probe too much. She hated when her family did that.

Her questions must have led Brooks to think he could ask some of his own because he leaned toward her again. This time his face was very close to hers as he inquired, "So what was the job you left?"

After a heavy sigh, she admitted, "I was a glorified secretary."

"A secretary," he murmured, studying her. "How long are you staying in Rust Creek Falls?"

"I've already been in town for a while, so I guess I'll have to go back soon. I work for Thunder Canyon Resort. I'm in the pool of assistants who handle everything to do about skiing. I had a lot of vacation time built up but that's gone now. I don't want to use all my savings because I want to earn my degree. Someday

I'm going to own a ranch and run a non-profit organization to rescue horses."

Brooks leaned away again and really assessed her as if he was trying to read every thought in her head, as if he was trying to decide if what she'd told him was really true. Of course it was true. A rescue ranch had been a burning goal for a while.

"How did you get involved in rescuing horses?"

"I help out a friend who does it."

Finally, Brooks took a few long swigs of his beer and then set down his glass. He looked at it and then grimaced. "I didn't even offer to buy you a drink. What would you like?"

"A beer would be fine."

Brooks waved down the bartender and soon Jazzy was rolling her finger around the foam on the rim of her glass. This felt like a date, though it wasn't. This felt…nice.

The music on the jukebox had stopped for the moment, and she listened to the chatter of voices, the clink of glasses and bang of a dish as a waitress set a burger in front of a cowboy.

Finally, as if Brooks had come to some conclusion, he swiveled on his stool and faced her. "If you had a job in Rust Creek Falls, would you stay longer?"

She had no idea where this was going since the town had few jobs to spare, but she told him the truth. "I might."

"How would you like to come work for me as my secretary and assistant?"

"I don't understand. You said you work for the vet practice in Kalispell."

"I made a decision tonight. There's only one way to

keep my father from running himself into the ground, and that's to take some business away from him. If I open an office here in Rust Creek Falls, I can take the load off my father and show him at the same time that he can feel confident handing down his practice to me, whether I marry or not."

She admired what Brooks wanted to do for his father. Would working for him move her life forward? She could learn a lot from him.

"Can I think about it, at least until tomorrow?"

"Sure. In fact, take a couple of days. Why don't you come along with me on my appointments to get a feel for my practice day after tomorrow? I'm going to have loose ends to tie up in Kalispell, but then you and I can spend the day together and you can see what my practice will involve."

When she looked into Brooks's dark eyes, she felt something deep in her being. In that moment, the world seemed to drop away.

They might have gazed into each other's eyes like that all night except—

Cecilia Clifton was suddenly standing beside Jazzy saying, "You should have come to the meeting. The town's making plans for the holidays." When her gaze fell on Brooks, she stopped and said a breathy "Hi."

Yes, Brooks could take a woman's breath away. Jazzy thought again about his offer. "I'd like to shadow you for a day and see what you do."

Brooks smiled and so did she. She had a feeling the day after tomorrow was going to be a day to remember.

Chapter Two

Two days later, Brooks pulled his truck to a stop in front of Strickland's Boarding House, a four-story ramshackle Victorian. Its once-purple paint had faded to a lavender-gray. Cowboys on the rodeo circuit had bunked here over the years, but right now, many of the folks from Thunder Canyon who had come to help were staying here. Melba and Old Gene Strickland cared about their guests in an old-fashioned family way.

He switched off his ignition, thinking he must have been crazy to ask Jazzy Cates to work for him. He really knew nothing about her except what she'd told him. He'd followed his gut instinct as he often did in his work. But that didn't mean he was right. After all, he'd been all wrong about Lynnette. He'd thought she was the type of woman who understood fidelity and loyalty and standing by her man. But he'd been so wrong.

He knew, however, he was right about opening the local practice and taking some of the workload from his father. After all, it was for the older man's best interests. Still…asking Jazzy to become involved in that undertaking—

She was so pretty with that blond hair and those blue eyes. When he'd looked into those eyes, he'd felt a stirring that had practically startled him. It had been a very long time since a woman caused *that* reaction. However, if he hired her on, he'd have to forget about her natural prettiness and any attraction zinging between them. He'd be her employer and he'd have to fix his mind on the fact that she was just a Girl Friday who was going to help him, maybe only temporarily. She might hightail it back to Thunder Canyon sooner than he expected. After all, Lynnette hadn't wanted to live in a small town like Rust Creek Falls. How many women did?

The wooden steps leading to the rambling porch creaked under his boots. He opened the front door with its glass panel and lace curtain and caught the scent of something sweet baking. Forgetting all about Melba's well-deserved reputation as a terrific baker, he'd picked up donuts and coffee at Daisy's Donuts, never thinking Jazzy might have had breakfast already.

Jazzy had told him the number of her room—2D, on the second floor. He climbed the steps to the second floor and strode down the hall to her room. He gave a double knock on her door and waited. Maybe she'd forgotten all about going with him today. Maybe she wasn't an early riser. Maybe she was down at breakfast. Maybe she'd decided going along with him today was tantamount to calf-roping!

She opened the door before he could push aside

the flap of his denim jacket and stuff one hand in his jeans' pocket. She was wearing an outfit similar to what she'd had on the other night, a snap-button, long-sleeve blouse and skinny blue jeans that molded to her legs. He quickly brought his gaze up to her face.

"I was running a little late," she said breathlessly, "but I'm ready."

She'd tied her wavy blond hair in a ponytail. Her bangs straggled over her brow. Forgetting she was pretty might be a little hard to do. "I brought donuts and coffee from Daisy's if you're interested."

"Oh, I'm interested."

They couldn't seem to look away from each other and her words seemed to have an underlying meaning. No. No underlying meaning. He just hadn't dated a woman in a very long time. He was reading too much into cornflower-blue eyes that could make a man lose his focus.

Brooks never lost his focus. Not since his mother had died. Not during his years at Colorado State. Not during his engagement. His focus was the reason his engagement had gone south.

"Let's get going, then. I have an appointment with Sam Findley at his ranch at seven-thirty to check on a couple of horses that almost drowned in the flood. One of them has PTSD and gets spooked real easy now."

"Were they hurt physically?" Jazzy closed and locked the door to her room, slipping the key into her hobo bag that hung from her shoulder.

"Sparky had a few deep cuts that have taken their good time healing. I want to make sure he hasn't opened them up again."

"Is most of your work with horses?"

"Lots of it is with horses and cattle because of all the ranches around here. But I do my stint in the clinic, too. Or at least I did."

At the end of Jazzy's hall, Brooks motioned for her to precede him down the steps. When she passed him, he caught a whiff of something flowery. Could be shampoo. Could be lotion. He didn't think she'd wear perfume for this little jaunt, but what did he know? Women mystified him most of the time.

Jazzy clambered down the steps in a way that told him she was high-energy. She went outside to the porch railing and stared up at the sky that was almost the same color as her eyes. She pointed up to the white clouds scuttling across the vista, hanging so low they looked as if a person could reach them.

"Isn't that beautiful? I never appreciated a day without rain as I do now."

She wasn't just pretty. She was gorgeous. Not in a highfalutin-model kind of way, but in a prettiest-gal-in-town way. He crossed the distance between them and stood at the railing with her.

"I know what you mean. I've never seen so much devastation. Half the town was affected. Thank God for our hills. The General Store, Daisy's and Strickland's were all on the higher side. The other side of Rust Creek is still recovering, and that's where we're headed." Standing beside her like this, his arm brushing hers, talking about the sky and the flood, seemed a little too intimate somehow. Weird. He had to get his head on straight and do it fast.

Jazzy gave him one of her quick smiles. He'd seen a few of those the other night at the Ace in the Hole.

Then she headed for the steps. She was a woman who knew how to move. A woman with purpose.

In his truck, he said, "You didn't wear a jacket. Even though we're having a bout of Indian summer, the morning's a little cool. Want the heat on?"

Glancing over at him, she motioned to the coffee in the holder. "If one of those is mine, that's all I need."

"Donut now or later?"

"One now wouldn't hurt."

He chuckled and reached for the bag in the back. "Cream and sugar are in there, too."

He watched as she poured two of the little cream containers into her coffee and then added the whole pack of sugar. She wasn't a straight caffeine kind of girl, which he supposed was all right.

"Dig around in the bag until you find the one you want."

She came up with a chocolate glazed, took a bite, and gave him a wink. "Perfect."

Brooks found his body getting tight, his blood running faster, and he quickly reached for his black coffee. After a few swallows that scalded his tongue and throat, he swiped a cream-filled donut from the bag and bit into it. Halfway through, he noticed Jazzy watching him.

"Daisy's Donuts are the best," she said a little breathlessly.

He was feeling a little breathless himself. Enough with the donuts and coffee. Time to get to work. Focus was everything.

Ten minutes later, Jazzy wondered if she'd said something wrong because Brooks had turned off the conversation spigot. He was acting as if the road was an enemy he was going to conquer. She supposed that was just as

well. Eating donuts with him had gotten a little…sticky.
She'd seen something in his eyes that had, well, excited
her…excited her in a way that nothing Griff had ever
done or said had. Downright silly. If she was going to
be working for Brooks—

She hadn't decided yet.

Veering to the left, Brooks drove down a rutted lane
that had been filled in with gravel. Yet, like on many
of the Rust Creek Falls streets, there were still a lot of
potholes. Paving crews had been doing their best, but
there was only so much money and only so much man-
power. Lodgepole pine grew on much of the property.
Larch, aspen and live oak were color-laden in October
with gold and rust. A couple of early snows had stripped
some of the leaves and there were still a bunch fluttering across the ground as they climbed out of the truck
and headed for the large, white barn.

"Does Mr. Findley run cattle?" Jazzy asked to soothe
the awkwardness and start conversation between them
once more.

Brooks responded without hesitation. "No. No cattle. Sam's livelihood didn't get affected like some. He's
a wilderness guide. Hunters and tourists stay at the
farmhouse, and he has two cabins out back. He stays
out there if he has women guests who would rather be
alone in the house."

"Sounds like a gentleman."

Brooks shrugged. "It's good business. A reputation
goes a long way out here. But then you should know
that. I imagine Thunder Canyon is the same."

"It is."

A tall, good-looking man with black hair and gray
eyes came to meet them at the barn door. Brooks intro-

duced Jazzy. "She's one of the volunteers from Thunder Canyon, but she's hanging with me today."

As Sam opened the barn door for Jazzy, he said, "Brooks has some kind of magic touch that I haven't had with Sparky ever since the flood." Sam shook his head. "I was the one who rescued him along with a couple of others, and maybe I hurt him without knowing it."

"Or maybe you just remind him of what happened," Brooks said easily. "Horses remember, just like cats and dogs. It's why a visit to the vet is so traumatic for some of them."

"He lets me feed him, but he won't take a carrot or sugar cube like he used to," Sam added regretfully. "And getting into his stall is a major undertaking. Are you used to being around horses?" Sam asked Jazzy, looking worried.

"Yes, I am. A friend rescues them and I help her out. I promise I won't go near Sparky if he doesn't want me near him."

"Do you want me to stay?" Sam asked Brooks.

"If you have things to do, and I'm sure you do, there's no need. We'll be fine."

Sam nodded, tipped his Stetson to Jazzy and headed back toward the house.

She watched him thoughtfully. "For a small town filled with gossip, I never heard anything about his tours while I've been here."

"Sam keeps a low profile, mostly advertises on the internet, attracts a lot of tourists from back East."

"Is he from here?"

"Nope, and nobody knows where he came from. He doesn't talk about himself much."

"Are you friends?"

Brooks thought about it. "We're something between acquaintances and friends."

"So that means you talk about sports and livestock."

Brooks chuckled. "I guess you could say that. You can add the goings-on in Rust Creek Falls, which is a topic of conversation for everyone. Come on, let's see Sparky. Sam has it rigged up so the stall doors open to the outside corral. He can come and go as he pleases."

"That's smart. Freedom's important to an animal that's been traumatized."

Brooks eyed her again as if trying to figure out who she was. *Good luck,* she thought. *She* was still trying to figure that out herself. Coming to Rust Creek Falls had changed her in some elemental way. Sure, in Thunder Canyon she had her family and her job. But she didn't want to live vicariously through her sisters and brother. She didn't want her family to be her world, and she certainly wanted her job to be more exciting than the one she had, or at least promise a better future. She couldn't get promoted without a degree, so she was going to get that degree.

"Let's take a look at Mirabelle first. Sparky will hear us and get used to us being around."

Jazzy had made a quick judgment about Brooks when she'd met him at the Ace in the Hole. The more she learned about him, the more she realized she'd been right. She'd been able to tell he cared about his dad. Now she could see he felt deeply about the animals he cared for. Just why did this man never intend to marry?

Mirabelle, a bay, was cavorting in the corral beside Sparky's. When she saw Brooks, she neighed.

Jazzy smiled. "She likes you."

"What's not to like?" He almost said it with a flirting tease, but then he sobered. "I've been treating her for a few years. One weekend, Sam had an emergency and couldn't reach my dad, so he rang up our practice. I was on call. Since then, I've been taking care of his horses. Gage Christensen's, too."

"The sheriff," Jazzy said, knowing Gage a little. They'd had a dinner date, but things never went any further.

"Yes."

"While I was at the elementary school working, I heard that he and Lissa Roarke are engaged." When she and Gage had dined at his office, his mind had definitely been elsewhere. Probably on Lissa, who'd flown in from the East to organize volunteers in Rust Creek Falls on behalf of an East Coast relief organization.

"So that's all around town, too?" Brooks asked.

"Lissa has been doing so much to get help for Rust Creek Falls that her name pops up often, especially with the volunteers."

"Gage went through a tough time after the flood, but he sure seems happy now."

"We had dinner," Jazzy said.

"Dinner? With Gage?"

"I stopped in at the sheriff's office to ask for directions. He and I started talking and one thing led to another. But his mind was elsewhere—I think it was on Lissa. That was soon after she arrived."

"You mean he asked you out because he didn't want to think about her?"

"Something like that, though I don't think he realized it at the time."

Brooks looked pensive as Mirabelle trotted toward him. He glanced at Jazzy. "Do you feel comfortable being out here with her?"

"Sure. Is there anything special you want me to do?"

"I'm just going to check her overall fitness, and make sure nothing insidious is going on. After a flood, all kinds of things can develop."

When Mirabelle came up to Brooks, Jazzy let the horse snuffle her fingers. That ritual completed, she petted her neck and threaded her fingers through the bay's mane. She talked to her while Brooks examined her. He checked one hoof after another, then pulled a treat from his back pocket and let her snatch it from his palm.

"She's the easy one," he remarked. "Now let's go check out Sparky."

Jazzy could easily see Sparky eyeing them warily, his tail swishing. "How do you want to do this?" she asked.

"We're going to sit on the fence and let him come to us."

"Do you think I should be sitting there with you, or should I go inside?"

"Let's give it a try. You can't force a horse to communicate with you. If I'm patient with Sparky, he usually comes around."

"He hasn't for Sam?"

"Sam was on a guiding tour when the rain started, but he got back in the nick of time. Sparky's tolerating Sam. But I think that has to do with the flood and the rescue, maybe a sense of abandonment. Animals have it, too."

Had Brooks felt abandoned when his mother died?

Had his father been there for him? Maybe that was at the root of their discord.

Brooks opened the gate at the rear of Mirabelle's corral, and they walked out.

"Sparky was watching us while we were tending to Mirabelle, so he knows we're here." Brooks went along the fence a little ways then climbed the first rung and held his hand out to Jazzy. She thought a man's hands told a lot about his character. Brooks's hand was large, his fingers long. Staring at it, she felt a little quiver in her stomach.

"Jazzy?" he asked, and she lifted her chin, meeting his gaze.

Zing.

Something happened when she looked into those deep, brown eyes. She took his hand and felt an even stronger buzz vibrate through her body. She could feel the calluses on his fingers that had come from hard work. She was curious about him and his life and she was afraid it showed.

They were both sitting on the top rung when Sparky froze midtrot and eyed them warily. He was a paint pony with dark brown swaths on his cream-colored coat.

"Now what?" she asked.

"We wait."

"Wait for what?"

"You'll see."

The horse did nothing for at least five minutes. He just stared at them. When Jazzy glanced at Brooks, she saw he wasn't the least bit impatient. Wasn't *that* a novelty. She shivered suddenly. The morning air *was* cool and she rubbed her arms.

"Are you cold?"

"The sun's warm."

"Not what I asked you." Brooks was wearing a denim jacket that fit his broad shoulders way too well. It was loose at his waist. She concentrated on the brass buttons on his jacket instead of contemplating other things about him.

He started to shrug out of the jacket and she clasped his arm, saying in a low voice, "No, really. I'm fine."

He chuckled. "You don't have to whisper around Sparky. He's not afraid of our voices, just of us getting too close when he doesn't want us to."

She felt herself blush, but she still held his arm because her hand seemed fascinated by the muscles underneath. Ignoring the fact that she said she was fine, he removed his jacket and hung it around her shoulders.

"You can give it back once the day warms up."

So he was protective, and…thought he knew best. What man didn't?

Although she protested, his jacket held his warmth and his scent. It felt good around her. She snuggled into it and watched Sparky eyeing them.

It happened slowly, Sparky's acceptance of them into his world. The horse tossed his head and blew out breaths. He lifted his tail and ran in the other direction, made a circle and then another that was a little closer to them. After about ten circles, he was only about five feet from them.

Brooks took a treat from his back pocket and held it out to the horse, palm up.

"Sam said he wouldn't take treats from him anymore."

"That's Sam. Sparky and I have an understanding. I

don't try to do anything he doesn't want me to do when he takes the treat."

"Rescue horses are often skittish like this," she said. "I mean, horses rescued from abuse, not floods."

"Trauma in whatever form has to be treated with kindness most of all, as well as a gentle hand and a firm determination to overcome whatever happened."

She'd seen that, working with the horses at Darlene's place.

It took Sparky a while but he finally came within a foot of Brooks's hand.

Jazzy didn't move or even take a breath.

Sparky snatched the piece of biscuit and danced away then looked back at Brooks to see if he had more.

With a smile, Brooks took another piece from his back pocket. "These get crushed by the end of the day, so you might as well eat them," he said in a conversational tone to the horse.

Sparky must have understood because he made another circle, but didn't dawdle this time. He snatched the biscuit and didn't dance away.

"How many times have you done this before?" Jazzy asked, completely aware of Brooks's tall, fit body beside her.

"Too many to count," he said, shifting on the fence but not moving away. "He and I go through this routine every time I come over. I'm hoping someday he'll see me and just trot right on up. I thought about buying him from Sam, but I don't think it's advisable to move him to another place right now.

"Can I look at you a little bit?" Brooks asked the horse.

Sparky blew out a few breaths but didn't move.

"I'll take that as a yes." Brooks slowly slid down off the fence, taking care not to jump too heavily onto the ground. The sleeves of his snap-button shirt blew in the wind, the chambray looking soft.

Jazzy was fascinated by man and horse.

Brooks found another crumb of the treat in his pocket and offered it to Sparky. The horse snuffled it up and Brooks patted his neck, running his hand under the horse's mane. He slowly separated the hair there and Jazzy could see a series of scratches and a five-inch long swatch that looked as if it had been stitched.

Although he pawed the ground, Sparky stayed in Brooks's vicinity.

"Come on down," Brooks said to Jazzy. "Slowly."

She eased herself off the fence.

"Stay there," Brooks warned her. "Let him catch more of your scent. Let him get used to you."

Rescued horses mostly needed to be cared for gently, then regularly watered and brushed when they'd let you do it. She'd never become involved with one quite this way before.

Brooks kept talking to Sparky and then gave her the okay to come closer. She did, feeling she was getting closer to Brooks, too.

Brooks gave her the last little bit of treat and she held it in her fingers. When she extended her palm, Sparky took it from her.

By then, Brooks was studying the horse's flanks. "He's looking good. Soon we can put him in the corral with Mirabelle and see how it goes."

"I think he'd like some company. Wouldn't you?" she crooned softly to the horse.

When she glanced at Brooks, he was watching her, listening to her, and her pulse raced.

At the end of the day, would he still believe he should hire her?

As Brooks drove to other ranches, Jazzy could see they were all recovering from the flood. In some fields, alfalfa had survived. Many ranchers had been soil-testing to find out what nutrients the flood had depleted. Some reseeded with fast-growing grasses, while others planted soybeans. All were trying their best to recover. Most were making headway.

She watched Brooks work with calves, with goats, with cattle. She helped however she could and realized she liked assisting him. They grabbed a quick lunch at the diner, talked about Rust Creek Falls and Thunder Canyon. Whenever their fingers brushed or their eyes met, Jazzy felt energized in a way she never had before.

At the end of the day when they were driving back to Strickland's, Brooks said, "I know I'm doing the right thing opening this practice. Dad's going to be angry about it, but in the end I think he'll thank me."

"You're doing something for his best interests, even if he doesn't see it that way. I guess roles reverse as parents age."

"And as children grow wiser."

She thought about that and all the advice her parents had given her. But she particularly remembered one thing her brother Brody had told her. He'd said, "You have to find the life you want to live, rather than settling for the life you've fallen into."

What life *did* she want to live?

Brooks drew up in front of the boarding house,

braked and switched off the ignition. Leaning toward her, he explained, "If you're my assistant, you wouldn't spend all your time in the field with me. Mostly what I need in the beginning is somebody to set up the office, make appointments, get the word out about the practice."

He paused for a moment, then honestly admitted, "At first I thought I'd been impulsive about asking you to work for me, but today I realized it really was good instinct that made me ask. You're great with the animals, Jazzy, and with the clients. You seem to be able to talk to almost anybody. That's a gift, and a great one in a receptionist. So if you take this job, you'll be a little bit of a lot of things—a receptionist, an assistant, a tech. What do you think? Do you want to work with me?"

Brooks was leaning toward her and she was leaning toward him. She felt a pull toward him and thought she saw an answering pull toward her in the darkening of his eyes. But if she accepted, they'd be boss and employee.

"Sure. I'd like that a lot."

Brooks extended his hand to seal the deal. When his hand gripped hers, she found herself leaning even closer to him. Whether he was aware of it or not, his thumb gently stroked the top of her hand, just for a moment.

Then he pulled away. "I'll wait until you get inside," he said gruffly. "Tomorrow I'd like to take you to the practice in Kalispell and let you talk to the office manager. Is that okay with you?"

"That's fine with me."

Looking into Brooks Smith's eyes, Jazzy realized their association was going to be more than fine. The thing was—he was a confirmed bachelor. So she'd better keep her head.

They'd *both* keep their heads because that's what bosses and employees should do.

Chapter Three

Jazzy had no sooner hopped into Brooks's truck Friday morning—he'd waited outside today—when she fastened her seat belt and turned to him. "I have a favor to ask."

Brooks cocked his head and his face said he was ready for almost anything. "I'd guess but I'll probably guess wrong."

"What makes you think you'd guess wrong?" she joked.

"Because I can*not* read a woman's mind. What's the favor?"

"I've been helping Dean at the elementary school when I'm not needed somewhere else, even though my carpentry skills are at a minimum. Still, I don't want to let him down. Can we stop over there on the way to Kalispell? I tried to call last night and kept getting his voice mail."

"He's engaged now, isn't he?" Brooks asked, obviously tuned in to the local chatter.

"He is. He bought a place with some land and he's just moved in with Shelby and her daughter Caitlin."

"Shelby works at the Ace in the Hole, right?"

"Yes, but for not much longer, she hopes. She's going to reapply for a job as an elementary school teacher once the school's up and running again."

"That could be a while."

"It might be, but that's what she wants to do. Anyway, he doesn't always answer his phone in the evenings. So I thought it might be just as well if we could stop at the school. I'll explain I'll be working with you, but I'll still help out around the school on weekends."

"You want his blessing?" Brooks didn't sound judgmental. He actually sounded as if he understood.

"Something like that."

"We can pick up donuts on the way and bribe him."

"Brooks!"

"I'm kidding. I often pick up donuts and drop off a couple of boxes for people who are volunteering. We all do what we can to say thank you."

After a stop at Daisy's, they drove to the elementary school property in a drizzling rain that had begun to fall. The low-hanging gray clouds predicted more of the same. Just what Rust Creek Falls didn't need.

At the school, the building crew had made progress, but it was slow going without money for materials, and work often had to stop while they waited for supplies. Today, however, Dean was there with a crew. They found him easily in the school library, building shelves. He looked up when he saw Jazzy and did a double-take as he spotted Brooks.

After Jazzy explained why they were there, Dean gave her an odd look. "You're not going back to Thunder Canyon?"

"I don't know when. For now working with Brooks will give me experience to open that horse rescue ranch I want to open someday."

"She's good with animals," Brooks assured Dean. To Jazzy he said, "If you're going to be a few minutes, I'll look around."

Perceptively Brooks probably sensed that she needed to convince Dean this was the best move for her. She nodded.

When Brooks left the library, Dean frowned. "What kind of relationship do you have with Brooks? I didn't even know you knew him."

"I didn't before the other night. But we hit it off."

"Hit it off as in—"

She knew she shouldn't get impatient with Dean. He cared as an older brother would. But his attitude was much like her family's when they second-guessed the decisions she made. "I know you think you have to look out for me while I'm here. But I'm thirty years old and old enough to know what I'm doing."

Assessing her with a penetrating glare, he asked bluntly, "Did you hook up with him?"

"No, I didn't hook up with him!" Her voice had risen and she lowered it. "He's going to be my *boss,* so don't get any ideas you shouldn't."

With a glance in the direction Brooks had taken, Dean offered, "Maybe *he'll* get some ideas he shouldn't."

Jazzy vehemently shook her head. "He's not like that."

Dean sighed. "I guess you'd know after a couple of days?"

"My radar's good, Dean. I know if I'm 'safe' around a man."

"Woman's intuition?" he asked with a cynical arched brow.

"Scoff if you want, but I believe in mine."

It was probably woman's intuition that had made her break off the relationship with Griff. Her instincts had told her he simply wasn't *the one*. There hadn't been enough passion, enough of those I-can't-live-without-you feelings. Something important had been missing.

"Okay," Dean conceded. "But be careful. I heard he's a confirmed bachelor with good reason. If you fall for him, you'll only get hurt."

She couldn't let this opportunity to find out information about Brooks pass her by. "Why is he a confirmed bachelor?"

After an assessing look that said he was telling her this for her own good, he kept his voice low. "He has a broken engagement in his history that cut him pretty deep. A wounded man is the worst kind to fall for. Watch your step, Jazzy, or you will get hurt. I don't want to see that happen. Not on my watch."

"I'm *not* your responsibility," she said, frustrated, and stalked out.

Ten minutes later with rain pouring down faster now, she and Brooks sat in his truck again, headed toward Kalispell. Dean's words still rang in her head. *A wounded man is the worst kind to fall for.* She wouldn't fall for Brooks. She couldn't. Besides, she didn't fall easily. Her relationship with Griff was proof of that.

Still, as she surreptitiously eyed his strong profile,

her stomach did a little somersault. To counteract the unsettling sensation, she remarked casually, "Progress is being made on the school, but it's going so slow."

"A ton of funds and a larger crew could fix that. But the way it is now, the elementary school teachers are going to be holding classes in their homes for a long while."

"The town has come a long way since I first arrived, though."

He nodded. "Yes, it has. The mayoral election next month should be interesting."

"Collin Traub against Nate Crawford."

"Yep. They butted heads trying to get the town back on its feet. Their families have a history of butting heads."

"A feud?"

"Some people say so. I don't know how it started. I don't know if anybody remembers. But because of it, the election is even more heated."

She wouldn't ask him who he was voting for. That was really none of her business. But other things were. "How did your clinic in Kalispell take the news you'd be leaving?"

He didn't answer right away, but when he did, he looked troubled. "I don't want to leave them in the lurch, and I won't. The other two vets in the practice understand why I have to do this. Family has to come first."

Her parents had always instilled that belief in their children, too.

Two hours later, Jazzy was still thinking about Brooks's broken engagement as well as everything she'd learned from the clinic's office manager about the computer programs they used, advertising and a multitude of other elements she'd have to coordinate to set up his practice. The rain had continued to pour as Brooks and the office manager had filled Jazzy in on what her job would entail.

Jazzy had worn a windbreaker this morning in deference to the weather and now flipped up the red hood as she and Brooks ran to his truck. He'd gone to her side with her to give her a hand up to climb in, but that meant he'd gotten even damper from the rain.

Inside his truck, he took off his Stetson and brushed the raindrops outside before he closed the door. Then he tossed it into the backseat.

"Where's your jacket today?" she asked.

"The same place yours was yesterday."

His crooked half smile and the curve of his lips had her thinking of other things than setting up his office. An unbidden thought popped into her head. What would it feel like to be kissed by Brooks Smith?

No! She was *not* going there.

Brooks looked away and she was glad because she was afraid he might read her thoughts. As he started up the truck, she said, "You need a name for the practice." It was the first thing that she could think of to say.

"I guess I can't call it Smith's Veterinary Practice, can I? That's what my father uses. Any suggestions?"

"Not off the top of my head. Once you pick a location, we might choose something geared to that."

"I like your ideas," he said simply, and she felt a blush coming on because there was admiration in his voice. When was the last time someone told her they liked her ideas? At work, she just did what was pushed in front of her. Sure, she offered suggestions now and then, but nothing that really mattered. Brooks seemed to make *everything* matter.

The rain poured down in front of them like sheets that they could hardly see through. Brooks didn't seem to be anxious about it, though. He drove as if he drove in this weather all the time, keeping a safe distance from whatever taillights blinked in front of them, making sure he didn't drive through puddles that were growing deep.

They were well out of Kalispell when he asked, "So you think you can handle setting up the office? The printing for flyers and business cards and that type of thing will have to be done in Kalispell, but we can accomplish a lot of it through email. I know this is a big job—"

Was he having second thoughts about her abilities? "I can handle it," she said with more assurance than she felt.

She must have sounded a little vehement because he cut her another glance. "I don't want you to be overwhelmed. There's a lot to think about. We can farm out the website design."

"I can do it. I know I can, Brooks. I've taken night courses that I thought might be useful at the resort, and I've never gotten a chance to use a lot of what I learned, including web design and graphics. I even took a course in setting up a small business in case I ever get the chance to start up my rescue ranch. I've put my life on hold for too long. By helping you, I finally feel as if I'm moving forward."

He was silent for a few moments, then asked, "Did you have other things on hold, other than your job?"

Was he fishing about her personal life? She could tell him about Griff—

And maybe she would have. But the water was moving fast along both shoulders of the road. As she thought about Brooks's broken engagement, how she'd told Griff she couldn't see a future for *them,* the truck suddenly dipped into a hole hidden under a puddle. The jarring jolt would have been bad enough, but a loud pop like a gun going off accompanied it.

Brooks swore and muttered, "I know that sound."

Their blow-out caused the truck to spin on the back tire until they faced the wrong direction. The vehicle hydroplaned on another puddle and they ended up near the guard rail on the opposite side of the road.

It had all happened so fast, Jazzy almost felt stunned, like she'd been on some amusement-park ride that had gone amuck. Her brain was scrambled for a few seconds until she got her bearings and realized they were half on and half off the highway.

Brooks unsnapped his seat belt and moved closer to her. "Are you okay?"

"I think so." Without conscious thought, she rubbed her shoulder. "We blew a tire?"

He nodded. "I'm going to have to change it."

"Oh, Brooks. In this rain? I can call Cecelia or Dean."

"There's no need for that. I've changed tires before. I've gotten wet before. It won't take long, Jazzy, once I get us set up right. Trust me."

Trust him. Could she? She didn't know if she could or not…yet. She'd be foolish if she trusted him on this short acquaintance. Yet she had seen enough to trust in his abilities, to trust that he'd do what he said he was going to do.

His gaze ran over her again. "Let me get us over to the shoulder on the right side of the road so I can take care of the tire."

"I can help."

"Jazzy—"

"We can argue about it or we can change the tire," she said adamantly, not accepting a macho attitude from him any more than she would from Dean, her brother or her dad.

"Are you going to tell me stubbornness is one of your virtues?" he asked warily.

"Possibly. Apparently we both have the same virtue."

He shook his head. "Let's get this done."

Jazzy was more shaken than she was letting on, and her shoulder *did* hurt. But she wouldn't be telling Brooks about it. Testing it, she realized she could move it, and she wasn't in excruciating pain. Those were both good signs. She could help Brooks and worry about her shoulder later.

Brooks managed to steer the truck around and with the thump-thump-thump of the blown tire, they made it to the right side of the highway over to the paved shoulder. Thank goodness the shoulder was wide enough that they wouldn't be in any danger as other vehicles passed.

Brooks touched her arm. "Stay here. I've got this."

But she, of course, wouldn't listen. She hopped out of the truck and met him at the rear of the vehicle.

He shook his head. "You're crazy. You're going to get soaked."

"So we'll be soaked together. I've helped my brother and dad change tires. I'm not inept at this."

He lowered the rear truck panel. "I didn't think you

were. Let me grab the spare and we'll get this done quick."

"Quick" was a relative term, too, when changing a tire in the rain. Jazzy had tied her hood tightly around her face and she felt bad for Brooks when his shirt became plastered to his skin. But he didn't complain and she didn't, either, though she was cold and shivery. That was so much the better for her shoulder because it was aching some. The cuffs of her jeans were protected by her boots, but from thighs to below her knees, she was getting soaked.

Twenty minutes later they were back in the truck with rain still sluicing down the front windshield.

Brooks reached in the back and took a duffel from the seat. "I carry a spare set of duds in case a calf or a horse drags me into a muddy field. It *has* happened. How are you under that jacket?"

Actually, the waterproof fabric had kept her fairly dry. "I'm good. Just my jeans are wet."

He switched on the ignition and the heater. "How's your shoulder?"

"Numb right now from the cold and damp."

He began unbuttoning his shirt.

At first she just stared at the tan skin and brown curly hair he revealed as he unfastened one button and then the next. For some insane reason, she suddenly had the urge to move closer…and touch him.

When his gaze met hers, her breath almost stopped. She quickly looked away.

She could hear the rustle of fabric…hear him reach into the duffel bag.

"Jazzy, take this."

Out of the corner of her eye, she could see he was offering her a hand towel.

"You need it more than I do," she managed to say, her eyes skittering over his bare chest.

"Wipe your face," he suggested. "Then I'll use it."

She took the towel and dabbed at her rain-splattered cheeks, the ends of her hair that had slipped out from under the hood. After she handed it back to him, her gaze went again to his completely bare chest, broad shoulders, muscled arms. Wow!

"Do you work out?" she asked inanely, knowing he'd noticed she'd noticed, and there was nothing she could do about that.

"No need to work out when I wrestle with calves, chop wood for my stove and repair fencing on my dad's property when he lets me."

"Do you have a house in Kalispell?"

"No. Because I fully intended to move back to Rust Creek Falls someday. I'm in one of those double condos on one floor. It's got everything I need."

She handed him the towel and watched as he dried his hair with it. It was sticking up all over. She wanted to run her fingers through it and brush it down, but he quickly did that and swiped the towel over his torso.

"Getting warmer?" he asked, with the heater running full blast.

"Yes. I'm fine. I can't believe *you're* not shivering."

"Hot-blooded," he said with a grin that urged her once again to touch him, test the texture of his skin, and see if there really was heat there.

Before she had the chance to act foolishly, he pulled a T-shirt from the duffel, slipped it over his head, maneuvered his arms inside and pulled it down over his chest. She could see denim protruding from the duffel.

"Is that another pair of jeans?"

"Yes, it is."

"You should change."

"I'm fine. Let's get you back to Strickland's and look at that shoulder."

"You're a veterinarian," she protested.

"I had some EMT training, too. Out here, you never know what you're going to run into. If you'd rather I take you back into Kalispell to the hospital—"

"No! I don't need a hospital or a doctor."

"Great. Then I'm perfect for the job."

After that, every time Jazzy glanced at Brooks, she envisioned his bare chest, his triceps and biceps and deltoids and whatever else she'd seen. He had tan lines from shirtsleeves on his upper arms. He had dark brown hair arrowing down to his belt buckle. He had a flat stomach and a slim waist and—

Okay, heating up her body wasn't helping her shoulder. In fact, it was starting to hurt a little more.

They didn't talk as he concentrated on driving and *she* tried not to concentrate on him. She thought about her sisters and brother and parents, and considered phoning them. She hadn't checked in for a while and they'd want to know what she was doing. However, should she tell them about her job with Brooks? She almost had to, because Dean probably would. Besides that, the news would soon get around to the other volunteers and some of them would be going back to Thunder Canyon. It was difficult to hide anything in a small town.

When Brooks pulled up in front of Strickland's, Jazzy said, "You don't have to see me in."

"I don't have to, but I'm going to. I told you, I want to check your shoulder."

"You're still wet. You'll catch cold."

He laughed. "Everyone knows you don't catch cold from the cold. I promise, this will be almost painless, Jazzy. I just want to make sure you're not really hurt."

Okay, so they were going to have to get this over with because he was persistent and stubborn. In a family as large as hers, she'd learned there was no point in arguing.

Once inside Strickland's, they climbed the stairs. Jazzy took out her key and opened her door. She'd already told Dean that Brooks was "safe," so why was she hesitating in letting him into her room?

Simple. He was half dry, half wet, and all imposing male.

Her room was small and the nice thing about it was it had a bathroom of its own. Standing by the single bed, Jazzy was very aware of it as Brooks came into the room and stood before her.

"I left the door open," he said. "I don't want you to think I have an ulterior motive."

He had left it open about six inches, and she realized how thoughtful it was of him to do that. She simply had to think about him as a doctor right now.

"Take your jacket off," he said gently.

At first her fingers fumbled with the zipper. Her nervousness was stupid. She had nothing to be nervous about. But unzipping her jacket, she felt as if she were letting him into her life in a different way. She shrugged out of it and hung it over the bed post. He took a step closer to her, and she suddenly felt as if she couldn't breathe. Her gaze locked to his for a few seconds, but then he directed his focus to her shoulder and reached out to touch it.

She thought she'd prepared herself. She thought this would be clinical.

The exam *was* clinical on his part as he kneaded around the joint and asked, "Does that hurt?"

"Some," she managed to say.

"Don't soft pedal it if it does."

"It's not that bad. Really."

As he felt along the back of her shoulder, she winced. His fingertips massaged the spot and she found that didn't hurt but felt good.

"You got bumped around and might have black-and-blue marks tomorrow. Put some ice on it for the first twenty-four hours, ten minutes on, half hour off."

"Yes, Doctor," she said with a slight smile.

His fingers stopped moving. His eyes found hers. The room seemed to spin.

No, not really. Couldn't be. But gazing into Brooks's eyes was like getting lost in forever. His hand was on her back now as he leaned a little closer. She felt herself swaying toward him.

But then he straightened. "Take it easy for the rest of the day."

Feeling reality hitting her straight in the face, she asked, "When do I officially start work for you?"

"Let's consider tomorrow the starting date. I've been talking to a real-estate agent and she'll have a list of places for me to look at. Would you like to go along to do that?"

"You bet."

"Unless you don't feel well."

"I'll be fine."

"Famous last words." He went to the door. "Ice the shoulder."

As he opened the door and went into the hall, she called after him, "Get out of those wet jeans."

She thought she heard a chuckle as he strode away from her room. She remembered his shirtless upper body. She remembered the feel of his fingers on her shoulder. She remembered the way his smile made her feel.

Working for Brooks Smith could be the biggest mistake she'd made…lately.

Chapter Four

The sun shone brightly in the brilliant turquoise sky as Brooks let himself into Strickland's Saturday morning, coffee and donuts in his hands. He'd found a property he wanted to show to Jazzy. She'd said yesterday she'd be ready anytime he was, but he hadn't wanted to waste her time, so he'd taken a look at three properties early this morning. He was confident one of them would work, but he wanted to see what she thought.

At the front desk, he greeted Melba who was shuffling papers into a file folder. She eyed the bag from Daisy's Donuts. "Jazzy didn't come down to breakfast," she told him. "Maybe she'll eat some of what you brought her."

He supposed Melba had seen him with Jazzy the past two days. The older woman watched over her guests with an eagle eye.

He climbed the stairs, glad he'd put lids on the coffee cups or he'd have sloshed it all over the box and donuts. He was just eager to show Jazzy the property, that was all.

But deep down, he knew the reason for his eagerness was more than that. When he brought Jazzy back here yesterday and examined her shoulder, he'd had to remind himself over and over again that it was a clinical examination. But he could vividly remember how she'd felt under his fingertips, the look in her eyes. They were attracted to each other and fighting it. Just how difficult was it going to be to work together?

Not too difficult, he hoped. They wouldn't have time for attraction, not if they were going to get a clinic up and running. So the sooner they looked at the property and got started, the better. It was silly, really, but he couldn't imagine doing this with anyone else. Jazzy was so positive and upbeat, so excited about new things. She understood the dedication it took to take care of animals, and she even admired it. Unlike Lynnette. She was so different from Lynnette. Jazzy wouldn't do anything half-measure. Dating Jazzy could be an unrivaled experience. More than dating her could be…

He thought about his dad's ultimatum. Marriage would be a solution. Yet after his experience with Lynnette, he couldn't even think about it.

It was a shame he couldn't erase the shadows of the past from his memory bank.

When he reached Jazzy's door, he shuffled the box into one arm and rapped. She didn't answer. Could she have gone out? Was that why she hadn't appeared at breakfast?

He rapped again. "Jazzy?" he called. "Are you in there?"

To his relief, he heard movement inside. Then Jazzy was opening the door, looking as if she'd just awakened from a deep sleep. Her blond hair was mussed around her face and she'd pushed her bangs to one side. She was wearing a raspberry-colored nightgown and robe over it, but she hadn't belted the robe and the lapels lay provocatively over her breasts.

He quickly raised his gaze to hers. "Are you okay?"

She seemed to come fully awake. Now she belted her robe, cinching it at her very slim waist. That wasn't a whole lot better, but she didn't know that. He'd just have to package his lusty thoughts away in mothballs. He was concerned about her and that concern must have shown.

"Tell me the truth, Jazzy." He didn't want some varnished description of how she was feeling.

"Can I tell you over donuts and coffee?" she asked. "That really smells good."

If she wanted coffee and was hungry, she had to be okay, right?

Without a second thought, he stepped inside the room. She moved over to the nightstand, clearing it of books and lotion. She set them on the small dresser.

After he settled the box on the nightstand, he pulled over the ladder-back chair while she curled up cross-legged on the bed. She was so natural…so unaffected… so pretty.

He opened the box of donuts, pulled out a chocolate-glazed one and handed it to her. "Tell me."

She wrinkled her nose at him. "As the day went on yesterday, I got more sore. Last night I couldn't get to sleep. It must have been about 4 a.m. when I finally did, and I guess I was in a deep sleep until you knocked. You should have called to warn me you were coming."

"You need a warning?"

She shrugged. "A girl doesn't like to be caught with her hair all messed up." She flipped a hank of it over her shoulder.

He laughed. "You look—"

She held her hand up to stop him. "Do *not* say fine. No woman wants to hear she looks fine."

"Then how about you look morning-fresh and pretty."

She'd been about to take a bite of the donut but she stopped and her eyes widened.

"What? You don't believe me?"

"I have sisters who look beautiful in the morning. They don't even get sheet wrinkles on their faces."

"You don't have any sheet wrinkles. Or *any* wrinkles at all."

Her skin was so creamy, he wanted to reach out and touch it. That was the problem. "You do have a few freckles, though. But I like those, too."

She blinked.

He could see he'd definitely surprised her, maybe even embarrassed her a little. He popped the lid off the coffee. "Sugar and cream, just like you like it." As he handed it to her, he asked, "So how sore are you this morning?"

"Just a little, really. I think some of it's from the seat belt."

That made sense.

"Do you feel like looking at a property I found? If you don't, we can do it another time."

"No, I want to go." She was about to lay down her donut, when he said, "Take your time. I told the real-estate agent I'd buzz her when we were on our way."

Jazzy suddenly got a determined look on her face,

and Brooks knew he was probably in for trouble. She pointed her donut at him. "Just because you're tall and strong and seem to know what you want in life, doesn't mean you can look at me as…fragile."

Now where had *that* come from? Honest to goodness, he just didn't understand women. "I don't."

She pointed her donut at him again. "You do. Maybe it's because you take care of animals, but you have some kind of protective streak. It's the same streak that argued with me about help with changing your tire, and being out in the rain and thinking I had to rest today. *You* were in the accident, too. *You're* not resting."

"I didn't bump my shoulder."

She lifted a finger and stroked the air. "Okay, point taken. Still, I'm not some damsel in distress. Got it?"

She was sitting there cross-legged on the bed—with mussed hair and a just-awakened look. Baser urges nudged him to move closer, to climb into bed with her…

As if he needed more proof she wasn't fragile, she said, "And I iced my shoulder yesterday like you told me to. I can take good care of myself."

Whether she could or couldn't remained to be seen, but he wasn't going to tell *her* that. After all, she'd left her home and her family and her job to come to Rust Creek Falls to help.

"You've been fighting having somebody look after you all your life, haven't you?" he asked perceptively.

She finished the rest of the donut and wiped her fingers on a napkin. "With a family as big as mine, it can't be helped. Everyone thinks they know best for everyone else. We do take care of each other, but sometimes it just gets very smothering." She licked one finger then picked up her coffee, took a couple of sips, then asked,

"Do I have time for a quick shower? I can be ready in ten minutes."

A woman who could be ready in ten minutes? This he had to see. "Go for it," he said and stood. "I'll go downstairs and wait. If Old Gene's down there, he'll want an update on how all the ranchers are doing. So if it goes a minute or two over ten, don't worry."

She hopped off the bed. "Ten minutes. Start timing."

He was still shaking his head, amused, as he went down the stairs. Jazzy was a bundle of…something. He wasn't sure what. She had energy and spirit and a smile that wouldn't quit. Maybe, just maybe, their partnership was going to work out.

Fifteen minutes later in Brooks's truck, Jazzy could feel his gaze on her and she knew she was just going to have to get used to that protective streak of his. It didn't feel so bad, really, coming from him—rather than from her brother or Dean or her dad. But she really was feeling better since the shower had loosened her up. Ice had definitely helped last night.

She was a bit surprised when he headed down Buckskin Road toward the creek. The properties in the lower-lying areas in the south part of the town had been the worst-hit by the floodwaters. Some of the properties directly north of the creek hadn't fared so well, either.

He pulled up in front of a refurbished one-story office. Another car was already parked there. When she and Brooks disembarked from his truck, an older woman in jeans, boots and a denim jacket nodded to them. Brooks introduced Jazzy to Rhonda Deatrick, who was a real-estate agent.

Rhonda handed Brooks a key. "Look around as long

as you want. You can drop the key back at the office when you're done. That way I won't interfere in your decision process."

He laughed. "In other words, you're not going to sway me one way or another."

She smiled. "You're just like your daddy. You know exactly what you want. So this will either work or it won't." She nodded to Jazzy. "Nice to meet you." She headed for her car.

"I guess she knows your dad?"

"Actually, she helped out my grandmother on some property issues. But Rhonda has a couple of horses my dad's taking care of, too."

"Everyone knows everybody here. But then Rust Creek Falls is even smaller than Thunder Canyon. Thunder Canyon used to be more like this, before money moved in with the resort and all."

They went up the short walkway that looked as if it had been recently power-washed. The building itself was sided in dark blue. Concrete steps led to the wooden porch with its steel-gray railing.

"Everything looks freshly painted and cleaned."

"From what I understand, there was a foot of mud in this place after the flood, so it was completely gutted and redone," Brooks explained.

"Was this a house?"

"No, it was a dentist's office. That's why it has a lot of good things going for it."

"The dentist didn't want to resume his practice?"

"Nope. He was near retirement age. He'd been renting the property for the past ten years. The owner was the one who decided to put it into tip-top shape again, and see if he could rent it to another doctor."

Brooks opened the door and stepped aside so Jazzy could precede him. She went up the steps, her arm brushing his chest. Even that swift contact affected her. The scent of his cologne affected her. Everything about him affected her.

Inside, everything was white. There was new dry wall in all the rooms, as well as new tile flooring.

"I think I'd leave the exam rooms in white for now," he said. "I can hang framed posters on the walls. But the reception area needs a coat of paint."

Jazzy examined the space. "An L-shaped desk would look good right there." She pointed to the wall across from them. "Or a counter. This would be pretty in a really pale blue, maybe with some stenciling around the ceiling."

"Stenciling?"

"Yes. You use a template and there are special paints. It's not difficult. I helped Mom do it in the kitchen. It could be on one of the walls or two of the walls, just around the doorways and windows. Whatever you decide. I'm sure there are plenty of animal stencils. It would look really cute. We can fill a basket with dog toys, another with cat toys."

"Everything in here has to be easy to clean," he reminded her.

She'd forgotten about that. "What's your dad's office like?"

"Practical."

"Animal owners are practical, but they want their pets to feel at home, too. Coming to the vet is often a traumatic experience. The more pleasant we make it for them, the more they'll be glad to come here."

"I like that philosophy. I'll try to have regular hours

here and make outside visits to ranches during specified times. I know there will be emergencies in both instances. Once I take patients away from Dad and he sees he doesn't have to work so hard, then maybe we can combine our practices. I can take over the majority of the work, and he can help out when he wants. Or else he can handle office visits and I can do the ranch visits, which are harder on him. It would be ideal. I think he just doesn't want to admit he can't do what he used to do."

"Nobody wants to admit that."

"Maybe so, but life is about change, even for, or especially for, older folk."

Before she thought better of it, she clasped his arm. "I think you're doing the right thing."

He covered her hand with his. "I surely hope so. Let me show you the rest. You can see the creek from the backyard."

Leading her into a hallway that led to the back of the office, he opened the door that went outside. The property had a huge backyard and beyond she *could* see Rust Creek.

"This is nice."

"I can imagine kennels out here and runs, which Dad doesn't have. Maybe eventually, if he doesn't give in to a joint practice, I could buy this place. Because of the flood, prices are down in this whole area."

"I imagine it could still be expensive."

After a long look at the creek, and then a glance at her, he said, "I've saved most of what I've made since I graduated. My rent's low, my scholarship paid for schooling. I've invested a lot of it since I've been working."

"How long have you been living in Kalispell?"

"Four years."

She saw something shadowy pass through his eyes and couldn't help asking, "But you really didn't intend to live there?"

"Life hasn't turned out as I expected."

She could keep silent, but that wasn't her way. Softly, she asked, "What did you expect?"

Again, he stared into the distance for so long a time she didn't think he was going to answer. But then his gaze came around to hers. "I expected to be married and practicing with Dad. But my fiancée broke our engagement and everything fell apart."

There was a lot of pain behind his words. From his broken engagement, or from his troubles with his father? If it was the broken engagement—

When she'd broken off her relationship with Griff, had it left this kind of pain with *him?* Brooks had confided in her and she realized that that confidence gave them an even more personal connection. If she reciprocated, their bond would grow. Unless he saw her in the same light as his fiancée. Right now, telling him about Griff just didn't seem to be the right thing to do, any which way.

They stood there in silence for a long time. Finally Brooks said, "I'm going to take it. This property seems perfect and I don't want to let it slip away. I can probably get all the paperwork done today. I'll start painting the reception area tomorrow morning."

"*You'll* start painting? I thought I was working for you now."

"Your shoulder's still sore and..."

The look she gave him must have stopped him. He

held up his hands in surrender. "Right. You don't want me to be protective. Do you want to paint, too?"

"Paint, and anything else that will help you get off the ground. If my shoulder's still sore tomorrow, then I'll decide what I can or can't do. Deal?"

A slow smile spread across his lips. "Deal."

But when they shook on it, Jazzy had the feeling she was agreeing to a lot more than a business arrangement.

The volunteers had carpooled for their initial drive to Rust Creek Falls, so Jazzy had left her car back in Thunder Canyon. She really didn't need it here because everything was within walking distance or she could catch a ride with someone. When Cecilia, who was also staying at Strickland's, dropped Jazzy off at Brooks's new clinic the following morning, she winked. "Have fun."

"We're going to work," Jazzy told her, for not the first time. She'd told Brooks yesterday, after they'd shaken hands on their deal, that she'd find her own way to the clinic.

"You can have fun and work, too," Cecilia reminded her.

But Jazzy was not looking at Brooks in any way other than as an employer. She simply was not. She was going to help him get his office ready. Period.

Glancing toward Brooks's truck, she wondered how long he'd been there. When she stepped inside his new office, she figured he'd probably arrived before dawn. There were tarps covering the floor, a flat of water bottles in one corner and a giant cup of coffee on the ladder.

"Did you have breakfast?" he asked. "I have donuts in the truck."

"I ate this morning. I knew I'd need some energy."

"How do you feel?"

"I feel like I should be here helping you paint. End of discussion, right?"

He gave her a slow smile. "Right. I only have one more wall. It would help me if you would do the trim around the windows."

"So I don't have to lift that heavy roller?"

"No. Because I think you'd be good at the detail work."

She laughed. "Very adept. Just point me to the brushes. What else is happening today?"

"Internet service will be hooked up tomorrow, same with phone. Equipment will also be delivered. I bought a secondhand desk at the used furniture shop and Norm said he'd actually deliver it today, even though it's Sunday."

"That's fast."

Brooks looked so tall and head-over-heels sexy this morning. He'd discarded his Stetson. His shirt might have seen a hundred washings because it was soft and a bit faded. He'd probably worn an old one in deference to the paint splatters he might get on it, she supposed. His jeans appeared worn, too, and fit him *so* well.

"I can't believe how fast this is happening."

"It has to happen fast for Dad's sake," Brooks said matter-of-factly.

"When are you going to tell him?"

"Once we're up and running. I don't want him to think it's something I won't go through with. I intend to present it to him as a done deal."

Brooks's cell phone buzzed. He took it from his belt and checked the caller ID. "I should take this. It's the Kalispell clinic."

Jazzy nodded and went to find the paint brush, but she couldn't help hearing Brooks say, "Clint can't handle it?"

He paused then added, "Yeah, I understand. Okay, it will take me about ten minutes." When he ended the call, he just stared at Jazzy. "I have to drive to a ranch outside of Kalispell, but I don't want to leave you here with this mess."

"No mess, just painting to be done."

"I don't like leaving you here without a vehicle."

"Strickland's is only a few blocks away. I can always call Cecilia or Dean if need be. Go, take care of whatever emergency has come up."

He came closer to her, so close she could see the rise and fall of his chest as he let out a long breath. He looked as if he wanted to…touch her and she wanted him to touch her.

His voice was husky as he said, "You're becoming indispensable."

Seriously she responded, "I don't think I've ever been indispensable."

He cocked his head. "That's hard to believe."

"In a large family, someone's always there, ready to step in. Sometimes when I get home after time away, it feels like no one's missed me. It's hard to explain."

Now he did reach out and touch her face, his thumb rough on her cheek. "I'd miss you if you weren't here."

"I shouldn't have said what I did." She could feel heat in her cheeks.

"You can say whatever you want to me, Jazzy. Sometimes it's easier to talk to strangers about the truth than to anyone else. Maybe that's why we hooked up at the Ace in the Hole."

Hooked up. But they really *hadn't* hooked up, not in that way. Still, she knew exactly what Brooks meant, and she couldn't help but say, "You're not a stranger anymore."

As soon as the words were out of her mouth, she wondered if she should have said them. Maybe he didn't feel the same way. But then his eyes darkened and he seemed as if he wanted to do more than touch her face, as if maybe he wanted to kiss her.

"No, we're not strangers anymore."

She tried to cover the excitement she was feeling, the heat and the speed of her racing pulse. "It's hard to believe we've only known each other less than a week. I feel as if I've known you longer."

"Much longer than a few days," he agreed, seemingly unable to look away. Then he appeared to remember he had something else to do, and someplace else he had to be. Whatever he'd been thinking and feeling got closed off. "I'd better get going. If there's any problem, call me," he reminded her.

There *was* a problem. She was much too attracted to Brooks Smith. *He's a confirmed bachelor,* she chastised herself. That was so hard to remember when he looked at her with his intense brown eyes.

Chapter Five

When Brooks stepped inside his Rust Creek Falls clinic—and he was beginning to think of it that way—he stopped short and just stared at Jazzy. She was sitting at the desk that had obviously been delivered when he was gone…in front of the wall that hadn't been finished the last time he'd looked. She hadn't just painted the trim, the baseboards, the door frames, she'd finished that wall, too. He didn't know whether to shake her or… *Go ahead and think it.* He wanted to take her to bed.

Not going to happen. He was her boss. They could never have a decent working relationship if they were involved, though that didn't keep him from imagining what it would be like—bringing her into his condo, undressing her slowly, leading them both into pleasure. He'd wondered more than once about her romantic past, and maybe it would come up because he had a question for her about it.

She stood when she saw him, all smiles. "I need to know if you're going to rely on word of mouth to get business, or if I should investigate some other advertisement opportunities." She had a pad and pen on the desk, jotting down ideas and the next items on a to-do list.

"Are we going to talk about what you did here this morning?"

"Not right now. There are more important things. I'll need to know your budget for advertising. Maybe you can tell me what's worked with the Kalispell clinic and what hasn't. What I think will serve you well now is to provide some kind of service that your father can't."

He'd been wrestling for the past few hours with recalcitrant cows. He'd washed off at an outside spigot but he still felt grimy, not at all as if he should be anywhere near Jazzy. Still, he approached her.

"You've given this a lot of thought."

"You want to succeed, don't you?"

"Sure, I want the practice to succeed, but more than that, I want Dad to see the success of this practice as a relief for him."

"So what service *doesn't* he provide?" she asked with that perky smile that made his whole body tense.

Keeping his mind on the question, he answered, "Dad doesn't do much work with small animals because he doesn't have time. He sets up office hours but then he gets called away. Ranchers can't bring horses and calves to him, so *he* goes to *them*. Traveling takes time. On top of that, Dad likes to gab. He spends a lot of time with his clients."

"Do you think that helps?"

"Sometimes it might, sometimes it might not. For instance, the first time I went to Sam's to help with his horses, we did spend a lot of time talking. I had to get a good feel for what was going on and what had happened to them. But since then, we talk very little, except if it's about the animals. Dad, on the other hand, would make a point of spending time with Sam with each visit."

"So what you're saying is that your dad's appointments aren't always on time."

"They're *rarely* on time. When he has office hours, his waiting room fills up and patients can be there an hour and a half to two hours before he gets to them."

"So that's a great place to start. His weakness can be our strength. We'll have to figure out a way to make sure you keep your office appointments, and I'll have to be certain I schedule them with the right amount of time."

"That envelope I gave you has a list of Kalispell services and the times that they schedule them. For instance, if you have a cat come in for an ear cleaning and a nail clip, that's a fifteen-minute appointment. A yearly check to discuss problems, get vaccinations, maybe flea treatments, would take a half an hour. Get my drift?"

"But I don't think it can be that cut and dried," she protested.

"You're right. After I get to know my patients, I can analyze their needs pretty accurately. I don't want to overcharge just because they take up my time, either. It's going to be a balance."

"I understand that."

He came around the side of the L-shaped desk unit. Jazzy was using a folding chair because the desk chair he'd bought wouldn't be delivered until tomorrow.

She ran her hand over the walnut finish on the desk.

"I like this. It's quality wood and sturdy. Your computer setup and printer should fit on here just fine."

"We'll see tomorrow. It shouldn't take too long to set up." He studied her. "But right now there's someplace I want to show you."

"Here in the office?"

"No. You've done enough work here today. I just want to show you something I like about Rust Creek Falls, and maybe you'll like it, too."

He was standing behind her as he looked over the desk and suddenly he couldn't keep from placing his hands on her shoulders.

She went perfectly still.

Jazzy felt warm under his hands. There was a comfort in holding her, but he felt a need to claim her somehow, too. Funny he should think of it that way.

He was grateful for her help, for her expertise in painting, for her caring about his practice and his dad. He cleared his throat. "Thank you for finishing this today, Jazzy. Tomorrow we can actually start setting up."

Releasing his grip on her, he stepped away.

She was silent for a moment but then her eyes sparkled in a way that invited him to get to know her better. "As soon as I wash up, I'm ready to go." Her voice was light.

They were going to keep everything between them *very* light.

As Brooks drove to the north of Rust Creek Falls, Jazzy recognized where they were headed—Falls Mountain. Tall evergreens were everywhere.

When the paved part of the road ended, Brooks

glanced at her. "This last stretch has been smoothed out some since the flood, but it could still be a little rough. Have you ever been to the falls?"

"I haven't. There just never seemed to be enough time to ride up here."

Brooks's truck bumped along the narrow road, which became a series of switchbacks under the never-ending groves of pines. One of the switchbacks led out onto a rocky point before doubling back. They could have parked there, she guessed, to get a view of Rust Creek Falls valley below, but they didn't. Brooks kept driving.

Suddenly they rounded a sharp turn and Jazzy could hear a tumbling, echoing roar. Mist wisped in front of them until finally as the sparkling sun reflected off shimmering water, she spotted the falls.

Brooks veered off the road to a safe spot and parked. "Would you like to get out? We can walk closer."

"Is it safe?"

"I promise I won't let you trip and fall over the edge." He grinned at her and she shook her head.

"I've done some hiking, I'll be—"

"Fine," he supplied for her and she had to grin back. There was something about Brooks Smith that made her want to dive into his arms. How could his fiancée have broken up with him?

After Jazzy climbed out of the truck, Brooks took her elbow as they walked toward the falls. They stood there a few moments in silence, listening to the fall of water, watching the mist puff up, admiring the late-day sunlight glinting off the cascade of ripples. They were standing close together. Brooks was still holding her elbow and it didn't feel protective as much as... close...intimate.

Because of that, because she wanted to know more about him, she asked, "Do you date much?" She knew what she'd heard from Dean, but she wanted to hear it from Brooks.

"I don't have time to date."

"If you did, would you?"

Instead of gazing at the falls now, he was gazing at her. "I don't know. Dating is meant to lead somewhere. I don't know if I want to go there for lots of reasons."

She knew she was prying but she asked, "Such as?"

The breeze and the mist wound about them, seeming to push them closer.

"Relationships require time, and I don't have it. Relationships require commitment, loyalty, fidelity and few people know how to give those."

She sorted that one out from all the rest. "You've put a lot of thought into it."

"Because I tried once and it didn't work."

Hmm, just what did that mean? Had Brooks's fiancée expected flowers, poems, rose petals and attention from morning to night? On the other hand, if Brooks really didn't know how to be a partner in a relationship...

She'd find out about the partner part.

"Did your mom and dad have a good marriage?"

"This is beginning to feel like the Inquisition," he grumbled.

"Sorry. I shouldn't have asked." She'd obviously pushed too far and she had a tendency to do that. She just hoped that she hadn't ruined their rapport.

But as if *he* needed answers, too, he asked, "What about *your* parents? Do they have a good marriage?"

She didn't mind talking about her parents. They were the epitome of what a married couple *should* be. "Oh, yes. They still hold hands. They enjoy being around each other. We can tell."

"You talk about it with your brother and sisters?"

She grinned. "Especially when we're trying to point out what we want for our futures. Three of my sisters are happily married. Incredibly lovesick." She sighed. "They sure have had more luck than I've had." Then, because she didn't want Brooks to think she was pathetic not being able to find anybody to love, she said, "But maybe that's because I don't like calf-roping. Maybe if I practiced, a cowboy would lift me out of the mud and he'd become my Prince Charming."

Brooks laughed. "That's a pipe dream if I ever heard one."

"Don't I know it. I limit my pipe dreams to achievable ones." And she could see, even if she'd begun to fall for Brooks Smith, that that road would lead nowhere. Whatever had happened to him had made him sure that a bachelor's life was the one he wanted.

What a shame.

The following morning, Jazzy was at the front desk, setting up the computer program. She glanced over at Brooks as he helped the delivery man move in more equipment and furniture. He was wearing jeans and a T-shirt today in deference to the work he was doing, and he looked good. All brawny, handsome cowboy.

They'd met here today and acted as if they hadn't shared those closer moments at the falls yesterday. But then she knew that was the way men acted sometimes. Her dad, especially, had trouble showing his feelings. And Brody, even though he was supposed to be a modern-day bachelor, didn't often put his into words, either.

In the reception area, Brooks pushed a few chairs into place and then asked Jazzy, "What do you think?"

"I think it's coming together. By tomorrow you should be ready to see patients. Later today, I'll see about putting the word out on local Kalispell sites. Getting the word out isn't always easy, but we'll do it."

Suddenly, a tall, thin woman with fire-red, frizzy hair burst into the office. "Brooks, what's going on here? I heard there was a bunch of commotion down here and came down to see myself."

With an expression of chagrin, Brooks turned to face the newcomer. "Hi, Irene. Have you met Jasmine Cates? Jazzy, this is Irene Murphy. She manages the feed department at Crawford's store."

"It's good to meet you, Mrs. Murphy." She wasn't touching this complication. She was going to let Brooks handle the woman and an explanation that might spread through the town like wildfire. Jazzy was an outsider, but Brooks wasn't, and the news would be better coming from him.

"I'm setting up a clinic here," he explained. "Buckskin Veterinary Clinic."

"You mean, you're like an annex to your dad's practice?" Irene inquired with a puzzled look on her face.

"No, I'm not an annex." Brooks didn't explain more.

Irene gave the place a good looking around, and her nose went a little higher into the air. "It looks like we'll have something to talk about at Crawford's today." Before Brooks could say another word, she'd swept out the door.

"Uh-oh," he muttered. "I'd better get hold of my father. She's the town crier. Nothing escapes her notice."

Brooks took out his phone and speed-dialed his dad's number. He frowned. "Voice mail. He must be out on a call. He leaves his phone in the car rather than carry it with him. That's a mistake for more than one reason. If he had it on him, at least he could dial 9-1-1 if something happened."

"Is there a reason he leaves it in his car?" Jazzy asked.

"He lost his phone once when he was tracking through a field and never found it again. When something happens once, Dad doesn't forget. He doesn't change easily, either."

When Brooks's face darkened, Jazzy suspected he was thinking about his broken engagement and his father's directive to get married or not join him in his practice. She didn't know how she'd feel if her parents gave her an ultimatum, like either get married or move out. But they'd never do that.

Nevertheless, she did often feel their concern that she hadn't met the right guy, that she wasn't settling down like her sisters, that she wouldn't have the grandchildren they were hoping for. That was a constant, steady pressure. She could only imagine the pressure Brooks was feeling with his dad's health being in danger. No wonder he wanted to do something about it.

A half hour later, Jazzy was proud of herself that she'd set up the computer program and it was ready to input patient data.

Brooks circled around the desk and leaned over her shoulder. "Great job, Jazzy."

Turning her head sideways, her face was very close to his.

"Thanks," she said, a little breathless. "Now I just have to round up some four-legged patients for you."

He didn't move away and she wondered if he liked the idea of being close as much as she did. His voice was husky when he said, "Once we get the sign up tomorrow, everyone will know we're here." He'd told her he had a friend who could paint a sign on short notice.

All of a sudden, the front door of the clinic banged opened and a tall, barrel-chested man, who was red-faced and almost looked as if he were breathing fire, came rushing in. "Just what in the hell are you doing?"

When Brooks straightened, he had a pained look on his face.

Jazzy asked, "Should I call the sheriff?"

"The sheriff?" the man bellowed. "*I* should be the one calling the sheriff. My own son is trying to put me out of business."

Now Jazzy saw the light. The irate man was Barrett Smith, Brooks's father. She couldn't believe he'd already gotten wind of what was happening here, but Irene Murphy must have put the word out.

Brooks rounded the desk so he was face-to-face with his dad, or rather boot to boot. "Calm down, Dad."

"Calm down? My own son is trying to humiliate me in front of the whole town!"

"I'm doing no such thing. I'm setting up a clinic to take some of your business away, so you're not working twenty hours a day."

"You've no right to interfere in my business."

"Just as you have no right to interfere in my life?" Brooks asked, a bit of resentment in his tone.

Uh-oh, Jazzy thought. This argument could really damage father-son relations. Yet she didn't feel she had the right to interfere.

"I'm older and wiser. I know best," Barrett blustered.

"You're older, but I don't know how much wiser. You won't see reason so I had to take matters into my own hands. We could see patients here today if we had to. We'll definitely be open soon, then you won't have to take all the night calls. If people in town start trusting me, we'll both have enough business."

"If they start trusting you? You're only four years out of vet school."

"Yes, and I know all the new techniques and new medications. Do you?"

"You think you know too much for your own good. If I put the word out that no one should come here, they won't. Then what are you going to do?"

"You don't have everybody under your thumb, Dad, including me. So just accept the inevitable and think about slowing down."

"The only time I'm going to slow down is when I'm in my grave." He pointed a finger at his son. "And you remember that. This isn't over, but I have someplace I've got to be." And with that, Barrett Smith left as brusquely as he'd come in.

"That went well, don't you think?" Brooks muttered as his father slammed the door behind him. Then he added, "Maybe marrying someone would be easier than all this!"

Jazzy felt bad for Brooks *and* for his dad. "You knew he'd be upset."

Brooks rubbed the back of his neck. "I should know

better than to get into a shouting match with him. It
never does either of us any good."

"You weren't shouting," Jazzy reminded him.

"My father thought I was. I wanted to break it to him
gently. Irene must have beamed it up to a satellite and
disseminated it through the whole town."

Jazzy bit back a smile at Brooks's wry tone. "Did the
two of you ever just sit down and *talk?*"

With a sad shake of his head, Brooks admitted, "No.
We haven't had a decent conversation in the past four
years."

She felt such a need to comfort him. "You know, our
families just want the best for us."

"What they think is the best for them is the best for
us, and that's not true. You asked if my parents had a
good marriage. They seemed to. They didn't fight. I saw
them kiss each morning before Dad left for work. He
wasn't around that much because he was always working, but my mother never complained. She warmed up
his suppers when he got home late. When he missed a
school event because of an emergency, she was there for
me and enjoyed it. She never wanted him to do anything
else. When she was diagnosed with cancer, my grandmother lived with us to help out, but I hardly remember that time. In some ways, it seemed to last forever,
and in others it was over in the blink of an eye. Three
months after her diagnosis, she died."

Jazzy came from around the back of the desk and
stood near Brooks. "I'm so sorry. I can't even imagine
losing a mom. My mom…well, she's our glue."

"That's exactly right," Brooks said. "Mom was our
glue, and when she was gone, it was as if Dad and I
had nothing else to hold us together. I spent time with

Dad with the animals just to be around him because I felt so adrift. But it's not as if we talked about what we were feeling…how much we missed her. It's not as if we talked about much of anything except the cases he took care of. When I wasn't with Dad, I was spending time with the horses. We had three and we boarded a couple of others. I could ride and forget for a little while. I could ride and eventually start to feel happy again. But I felt guilty when I felt happy."

"I don't think that's so unusual. Did you get over the guilt?"

"Eventually, but my dad… After my mom died, he changed. He became more rigid…harder. Sometimes I thought he expected perfection and I just never lived up to that. Now I think, like you said, he just wanted the best for me."

"So when you were a teenager, did you rebel?"

"Nope. I didn't want to give him a hard time. I wanted to keep the waters smooth. I played sports, told myself I didn't care if he was at my games or not. I got scholarships and that seemed to make him happy. So we had a tentative peace until everything went south with Lynnette and I felt as if I had disappointed him all over again."

Jazzy was more curious than ever to find out what had happened with his broken engagement, but he didn't seem to want to talk about it. In fact, he turned the tables on her.

"So did you rebel when you were a teenager?"

"I put a few pink streaks in my hair, got a tattoo, but that was about it."

"A tattoo?"

"It's a butterfly," she said. "But it's not someplace

that usually shows." She wasn't being provocative, but she saw him glancing at her arms. Maybe she hadn't meant to be provocative, but his eyes got that dark look again.

"There's much more to you than meets the eye," he said as if that wasn't a good thing.

"You like simple women?" she asked.

"I like women who are honest."

That gave her food for thought. She was about to follow up and ask him if Lynnette had been *dis*honest, but her cell phone played, announcing a call. She'd laid it on the counter beside the computer. Now she reached for it and saw it was her sister.

"Family," she said. "I'd better take this."

"Go ahead. How about some lunch? I'll go get take-out at Buffalo Bart's Wings To Go."

"That would be great."

Brooks gave her one last look before he grabbed his denim jacket from a chair and left the office.

"Hey, Jordyn," she said as she answered her phone. "What's up?"

"Mom told us you took a real job in Rust Creek Falls with a veterinarian. What's he like?"

Leave it to Jordyn to hone in on that.

"He's a veterinarian," Jazzy said evenly, to stop her sister from wandering further.

"How old?"

"He's twenty-nine."

"Ooh, and you just turned thirty not so long ago. Same age. Now give me the real details. Is he tall, dark and handsome?"

"He's tall," Jazzy teased. "And he's cowboy handsome. He's really great with animals, and he's a...gentleman."

"Are you falling?"

"No, of course not. I'm working for him."

"Those two things *aren't* mutually exclusive," Jordyn concluded.

"He's a confirmed bachelor."

"Uh-huh."

"And his life is complicated right now. He and his dad are arguing and—"

Jordyn cut in, "I hear something in your voice I never heard when you talked about Griff."

Out of all her family, Jordyn had probably been the least enthusiastic about her relationship with Griff. Maybe she'd sensed Jazzy's uncertainty about it.

"I'm working for Brooks," she said again. "Let's leave it at that. How are Mom and Dad?"

"They're fine. So is everybody else. But we're concerned about you. Are you giving notice to Thunder Canyon Resort?"

Wasn't *that* a good question?

"I should know in another week or so. I like working with Brooks and the animals. It's great practice for that horse-rescue ranch I want to start."

"You've given up on the business degree?"

"No, but for now, I don't want to plan. I just want to go with the flow. I'm tired of trying to meet other people's expectations of what my life should be."

"You're mad at the family because they wanted you to marry Griff."

"I'm not mad. I just got exasperated and tired of being watched over. I want my own life. I don't want to make finding a guy a priority because my family wants it for me. Do you know what I mean?"

"I know exactly what you mean. You want Prince Charming to drop out of the sky and land right at your feet."

"Jordyn—" This sister *could* be just as exasperating as the others.

"I get it, Jazzy, believe me, I do. And whatever you want to do, you know you have my support. So take a picture of this veterinarian with your phone and send it to me. I'll decide if he's Prince Charming material or not."

Chapter Six

On Friday, Jazzy printed out Mrs. Boyer's bill as the woman stooped to her beagle, patted a chocolate patch on his head and cooed, "You're going to feel better soon. I'll take good care of you." She looked up at Jazzy as Jazzy told her the amount of the office visit and waited as the woman wrote out her check.

It had only been a few days and Buckskin Veterinary Clinic was already seeing clients. Brooks had put a sign in the window that they were taking walk-in patients, and that had helped business, too.

"You know, your clinic is going to be convenient for me," Mrs. Boyer said. "Barrett is hard to get a hold of in an emergency. And it will be nice to have a practice that focuses on the smaller pets, too."

"I'm glad you decided to give us a try," Jazzy said sincerely.

Brooks came into the reception area from the back, carrying a bag. He handed it to Mrs. Boyer, a brunette in her midforties, who seemed to love her beagle like a child. "If Hilda won't take the whole pill," Brooks explained, "you can open the capsule and sprinkle it on her food. Just mix it in. It's supposed to have a liver and beef taste."

Mrs. Boyer laughed. "Hilda will eat almost anything."

"If anything comes up between now and your follow-up appointment, just give us a call."

"I was just telling Jazzy it's such a relief to know I can get a hold of you on short notice."

Jazzy and Brooks had made a pact that they wouldn't bad-mouth his dad, or say anything derogative about his practice. This was about building up Brooks's practice, and providing service to their clients. If they did that well, they would be successful.

"I saw your father at the General Store," Mrs. Boyer went on, glancing at Brooks. "I didn't know if I should say anything, but he was looking a bit peaked. When he left, one of the men he'd been talking to said Barrett had been complaining because some of his clients were coming here."

"We're just trying to provide an alternative to Dad's practice," Brooks explained. "I think the area has room for both of us."

Hilda began to whine. She obviously wasn't getting the attention she thought she deserved.

"I'd better get Hilda home. I understand we could have bad weather later today, rain into sleet. I think I'd almost rather see snow than more rain."

"A lot of other folks here would say the same thing," Brooks agreed.

After Mrs. Boyer deposited her checkbook in her purse, she led Hilda out the door.

As soon as the woman left, Jazzy turned to Brooks. "Maybe you should have a talk with your father."

"You saw what talking with Dad is like. It just raises his blood pressure."

"But if he's not looking well—"

"Jazzy, he won't listen to me."

"Do you think your practice really is starting to affect his?"

"After just a few days, it's hard to believe. Maybe he's seeing something that isn't there. He's never had much time for small animals. Most people here call our practice in Kalispell for their dogs and cats and bunnies. But if he's heard people are coming in here to us, maybe it's a psychological thing. I don't know. I just know the two of us can't seem to have a conversation about anything that matters, not without his temper— or mine—flaring."

"I haven't said one bad word about his practice," Jazzy assured him.

Brooks put his hand on her shoulder. "I know you haven't. Thank you for that. I want to do this fair and square."

The fact that Brooks was a man of integrity drew Jazzy to him as much as everything else about him. His hand on her shoulder felt warm. In fact, she could feel the heat from it all through her. Every time they were together, they seemed to have a rapport that went beyond words. She understood him a little better now since he'd told her about his childhood and about his broken engagement, though she still wondered why he'd broken up with Lynnette, or why she'd broken up with him. However, looking into his eyes right now, she didn't care at all about his past, just about being with him.

"You did a great job getting the word out about the practice through Dean and the other volunteers at the elementary school," Brooks said with appreciation. "I think that's made a difference. Are you still volunteering there on Sunday?"

She'd told Dean she'd still help out when she could, so she didn't mind giving up her day off to keep her word. "Yes, I am. I don't know how much help I'll be, but Dean says they can use anybody who knows how to swing a hammer."

"You've had practice swinging a hammer?" Brooks's hand still rested on her shoulder.

"Sure. Abby, Laila, Annabel and Jordyn never wanted to get dirty so I'd help Dad with his at-home projects like the shed in the backyard, or even work on the stalls and in the barn. I really am a Girl Friday. I can do a little bit of everything."

"You're proving that," Brooks said, gazing into her eyes.

When Brooks looked at her like that, her tummy did flip-flops, her breath came faster, and sometimes she even felt a little dizzy. It happened at the oddest moments—after he treated a little patient, when they were sharing hot wings over lunch, when he dropped her off at Strickland's. She wondered if that zing in the air whenever they were together was evident to anyone but her. She wondered what he thought about it.

He's a confirmed bachelor, she warned herself again. No sooner had she taken note of the warning, than

Brooks dropped his hand from her shoulder. "I'm thinking about helping out over there on Sunday, too."

"Really?"

"Don't sound so surprised. I told the Kalispell practice I'd be on call for them, but I know how far behind the elementary school is on their progress. It can't be easy for the teachers to be having classes in their homes. I think they're going to have more than the usual volunteers this weekend. I spoke to Dallas Traub from the Triple T as well as Gage Christensen last night. They're going to be at the school, too." He paused then went on, "You said you had dinner with Gage and it didn't go well. Is it awkward when you see him now?"

Was Brooks fishing to see if she might still be interested in Gage? If he was, he could put those thoughts to rest. "No, it's not awkward. We had dinner and that was that. He's a great guy. When anyone sees him with Lissa, it's obvious they're in love. I'm glad he's happy."

Just like her sisters were happy. Just like Willa and Shelby were happy. Sometimes Jazzy wanted what they had so badly that it hurt. Sometimes she could hear her biological clock ticking. Sometimes true love seemed to be a far-away dream that was never going to come true, at least not for her. She thought coming to someplace like Rust Creek Falls, she would stop the constant reminder. Maybe something was lacking in her that she couldn't find the *one,* that Mr. Right might simply not be out there for her.

The phone on the desk rang and she was glad for the interruption. However, before she picked it up, she studied Brooks. "I still think talking to your dad might be a good idea."

But Brooks shook his head. "I've never met a man

more stubborn than my father. He's solid rock once he's made a decision. But I will call his friend Charlie and ask him to keep an eye on Dad for me." He motioned to the phone. "Now see if we just picked up another client."

Brooks was a good man, she thought as he headed for the back of the clinic.

And a man who never intends to marry, she warned herself again as she picked up the phone.

It never should have happened.

Jazzy's dad had taught her to wear gloves when handling wood products. She usually did. But today, with Brooks working with her side by side, she didn't seem to have her head on straight. So when the two-by-four slipped and the splinter cut her, she knew it went deep.

Brooks was beside her in an instant. "What happened? Are you all right?"

"I'm fine," she said, unable to keep from grimacing in pain. "It's a splinter, that's all."

Brooks's steady gaze didn't waver from hers. He took her hand in his and saw the injury immediately. "I'm sure someone has a first-aid kit."

"Don't make a big deal of it."

"Jazzy, it needs to be looked after. Do you always try to fade into the woodwork and pretend everything's okay?"

Brooks's words shocked her somewhat until she realized they were sort of true. At home, she didn't want to cause anyone any trouble. It was simple as that. That's why she'd dated Griff as long as she had, even though she'd known there wasn't enough passion there. Her family had liked him. He'd come to dinner. He talked sports with her dad. Her parents had liked the fact

that his sporting-goods store was doing so well and
he was financially secure. She hadn't wanted to upset
the family applecart. She'd wanted to be on the road
they'd dreamed for her, and she'd dreamed for herself.
But Griff hadn't been right. Pretending she was happy
hadn't been right. Always standing in the background
hadn't been right.

"That's what I do, I guess," she admitted.

"Let me see if I can get it out without a tweezers,"
he suggested. Taking a close look at it, he manipulated
it a little, then pulled it out. "I think I got it all, but you
really should ask Dean if he has a first-aid kit and put
some antiseptic on it."

Brooks was close enough to kiss. He was close
enough for her to see the tiny scar above his eyebrow.
His caring and his attention were like a balm that she'd
needed for a couple of years and hadn't even known it.

She heard the titter of laughter across the room and
glanced at two volunteers who were eyeing her and
Brooks. Uh-oh. She didn't want any gossip starting
about the two of them.

Spotting a couple of other volunteers glancing their
way, too, she sighed. Did Brooks notice how they were
becoming the center of attention? Before he could, before any of it could get out of hand, she backed away
from him and said quickly, "I'll find Dean and get this
taken care of."

Her sudden agreement seemed to surprise Brooks.

She hurried to the hall. Dean was there and when he
saw her, he scowled! What was that about?

Approaching him, she asked, "Where do you keep
the first-aid kit? I have a splinter I'd like to bandage up."

"You can't leave it in."

"Brooks took it out. I just want to put antiseptic on it."

Taking her by the elbow, Dean guided her up the hall to a bathroom. "We've got running water in there now. Wash it with soap. I'll bring the kit in."

"To the girls' bathroom?" she asked with a laugh.

"It's the only one working. We do what we have to do."

With another smile, she went into the bathroom and did as Dean suggested. A few minutes later he was there with a plastic box. He removed a bottle of antiseptic and a tube of cream.

"I hope you know what you're doing," he said.

"I'm making sure my hand doesn't get infected."

"Don't play dumb with me, Jazzy. You don't do it very well."

She supposed that was a backhanded compliment. "What's the problem, Dean? Every time you look at me today, you're frowning."

"That's because there's been little ripples around you and Brooks today."

"Speak English, okay? What kind of ripples?"

"Whispers, under-breath comments like, 'Doesn't she work with him now? Maybe they're more than boss and employee.'"

"And you listen to gossip?"

"Of course not. That's why I'm asking you. Are you just Brooks's assistant or are you more than that?"

"I'm his assistant," she snapped. Then seeing that this was Dean, and remembering all the times she'd spent with Brooks over the past two weeks—the conversations, the lunches, the concern for his little patients, as well as his big patients, she added, "And his friend. You know how it is, Dean. You work with some-one all those hours and you talk about family, friends. You become closer than just two colleagues who push papers around."

"You're sure this hasn't gone beyond friends?"

"It has *not*."

"I spoke with Brody. He said they all know you're working with Brooks, though they don't know much about him."

"Jordyn does. She and I had a conversation about it. I don't want my family thinking up stories about the two of us any more than I want anyone here doing it. I wish everyone would just stop worrying about my life and concentrate on their own. You're going to be mar-ried and have a beautiful family, a wife who's going to be a teacher here, a little girl to love. Isn't that every-thing you've always dreamed of?"

"Yes, it is, actually. I want the same thing for you."

"When you want it for me, it feels like angst. It feels like something I have to live up to. I want to fall into it, not live up to it. I want to follow my bliss and let it lead to my happiness."

Dean started to smile.

"Please don't laugh. Over the past couple of years, I've found that the more I tried to control my life, the less control I had. So now, here, I'm taking what comes day by day. I'm going with the flow. I'm adopting an attitude of seeing a glass more full than more empty. And good things are happening. I lucked into this job with Brooks."

"Does it pay as much as Thunder Canyon?"

"Almost. So please stop being concerned for me, and please stop passing your concerns onto my family.

I'll talk to each one of them individually over the next few weeks. I'll make them understand that being here is right for me."

"You do have a new softness about you, a new mellowness. Does Brooks do that for you?"

"I don't know. I haven't thought about it. Does Shelby do that for you?"

"Yeah, she can, when I've had a bad day. Instead of being all grumpy or silent, she gets me talking and I get back on an even keel. You're still staying at Strickland's, right?"

"Right. Melba is giving the volunteers a good deal on rent, so I'm still saving most of what I'm earning. I'm fine, Dean."

Brooks knocked on the bathroom door and called, "Jazzy?"

"We're in here. It'll soon be a crowd."

Brooks laughed as he opened the door and saw Dean. "What do you think? Do we need to rush her to the emergency room in Kalispell?"

"Nah, I think she'll live."

"You two better think up a new routine," Jazzy muttered. "Something that will make me laugh instead of cry."

At that, they all laughed.

"Okay, I'll take my kit and go." Dean headed for the door.

As soon as the swinging door slapped behind him, Brooks moved closer to the sink where Jazzy stood. "All fixed up?"

"Ointment and a bandage. I'm good to go."

"Are you? Or is the gossip a problem for you?"

"I just don't want the wrong thing getting back to my family. I don't want to cause them stress and worry."

"I understand that. But you have to shut off the gossip. In a small town, it could ruin your life." He took her hand. "We have nothing to hide, Jazzy."

No, they didn't. Not yet. The business relationship was front and center. But she wondered about the other part of their relationship—the heat, the quivering excitement, the pull neither of them could deny. Yet Brooks was trying to deny it. Again she wondered if that was for her sake...or for his.

"Are you still going to be able to work okay, or do you want me to take you back to Strickland's?"

"I can work just fine."

Brooks's cell phone buzzed and they both glanced at the holster on his belt. "I have to get this," he said. "It could be the clinic."

"If you need to make a quick exit, I can get a ride home with Dean, no problem."

"Let's find out." Brooks checked caller ID and frowned. "It's Charlie Hartzell." Brooks answered quickly. "What's going on, Charlie?"

Jazzy watched the color drain from Brooks's face, watched his back straighten, his shoulders square. "When did this happen?" There was a pause.

"Thank God you were there," Brooks breathed. "I'll head to the hospital now. I'll meet you there."

After Brooks clicked off his phone, he said to Jazzy, "Dad collapsed. Charlie thinks it was a heart attack. He's on the way to the Kalispell hospital. I've got to get going."

He'd already started moving and Jazzy walked after

him, catching his arm. "Do you want me to go with you?"

His voice was gruff. "You don't have to do that."

"I want to, Brooks. You should have someone there... for *you*."

His eyes got that deeply dark intensity that she was beginning to understand meant he was experiencing deep feelings he didn't share. All he said was, "I'd appreciate that."

Fifteen minutes later—Brooks's foot had been very heavy on the accelerator—they walked into the hospital, not knowing what they'd find inside.

Much later that day, Brooks and Jazzy sat in the waiting room. Charlie had left and Jazzy was glad she'd come along with Brooks so he'd have somebody with him. The lines on his face cut deep, his expression was grim and tension filled his body. She could tell when she sat next to him. She could feel it when his arm brushed hers.

Brooks suddenly muttered, "I never should have had those arguments with him. I should have stayed detached and calm."

"He's your father, Brooks. How can you stay detached?"

"I've pretty much done it the past few years, and I regret that, too. I feel so guilty about all of it. If anything happens to him—" He shook his head. "Before they took him in for the procedure, I didn't even say what I should have."

That he loved his dad? Those words were sometimes hard to get out, especially in an emergency situation when time was limited and medical personnel were buzzing around.

Jazzy had been part of this push to get Brooks's new practice up and running quickly, and she felt partly responsible for everything that had happened. Maybe if they had handled it all differently, Brooks's dad wouldn't be in the hospital. She laid her hand on Brooks's arm, knowing nothing she said would ease what he was feeling.

A nurse came into the room and said to Brooks, "Your father has been taken to his room. Dr. Esposito would like to see you there. Just follow me."

Although Jazzy had stayed in the background until now, she knew it was hard to absorb everything a doctor said in this type of situation. She asked Brooks, "Do you want me to come with you?"

He didn't hesitate. "I'd appreciate that."

When they stepped into Barrett Smith's room, Jazzy thought Brooks's dad looked ten years older than he had when she'd seen him last. He was hooked up to an IV and he was scowling.

Dr. Esposito, with his wavy black hair and flashing brown eyes, glanced at Barrett's chart and then up at the two of them. "You're Barrett's son?" he asked Brooks.

Brooks nodded and shook the man's hand. The doctor glanced at Jazzy. "And she is?"

"She's a friend of mine," Brooks said.

The doctor eyed Barrett. "It's up to you whether I should discuss this in front of her."

Barrett waved his hand. "After a man goes to the hospital, nothing's private. What's it matter?"

"Is that permission to let her stay?" the doctor asked Barrett.

"Hell, yes," the older man said. "Just get on with it. I want to go home."

The doctor's arched brows and patience said he'd seen this reaction before. "Your father experienced a myocardial infarction. Fortunately, not a severe one. We inserted a stent in a blocked artery."

"Is that going to take care of the problem?" Brooks asked.

"It will take care of the problem for right now. We're of course monitoring him and he'll have to get checkups. I'll set up a follow-up appointment when he's released. But as I was telling your father, I believe his attack was brought on by several factors—exhaustion, overexertion and a lifestyle not conducive to heart health."

Silence reigned in the room.

"What does he have to do to stay healthy?" Brooks asked.

"He has to change his habits if he wants to live a long life."

"I'm here," Barrett said. "Don't talk to them as if I'm not. I have a veterinary practice. I eat when I can. I work because the work's there."

"Yes, well, that doesn't mean you can't make adjustments," the doctor said. "I'll also be putting you on medication—one is a blood thinner and the other is to help lower your cholesterol."

"I hate taking medicine," Barrett grumbled.

"Dad, you'll do what the doctor says."

Barrett crossed his arms over his chest and looked very much like a rebellious teenager.

Dr. Esposito remained passive. "I'll be talking to your father again before he's released, probably tomorrow. I want to monitor him overnight. I also want to set him up with a consultation with one of our nutritionists about diet."

"I already know," Barrett said. "It's all over the TV and news. But I'm *not* going to turn into a vegetarian."

"You don't have to turn into a vegetarian," the doctor protested. "But you *do* have to practice moderation. I'll leave you to talk to your son." He said to Brooks, "If you have any questions, I'll be on this floor about another half hour or so."

After the doctor left, Brooks said to his dad, "You have to take care of yourself. You have to let me take over the practice."

Barrett looked up at Brooks, mutiny in his eyes. "No, I don't. This is just a little setback. I'm not giving up my practice until you're settled down."

A nurse bustled into the room to check Barrett's IV and they all went quiet. But as she began to take Barrett's blood pressure, Barrett waved his son away. "Go! Go home. I need to rest. I'm going to be just fine."

Brooks looked as if he wanted to go to his father, sit beside him, convince him to do what was best. But Jazzy knew Barrett was in no mood for that now. She gently touched Brooks's elbow. "Let's let him rest for now. We can come back."

She could see the torn look on Brooks's face. But when he looked at his dad and Barrett stared back defiantly, Brooks gave a resigned sigh. "All right, we'll leave for now. But I'll be back."

"Famous last words," Barrett muttered. "Go take care of your own life and let me take care of mine."

Outside the room, Brooks stopped in the hall. He

suddenly erupted, "He makes me want to put my fist through the wall."

"You don't need a broken hand on top of everything else," Jazzy reminded him.

Brooks studied her, went silent, studied her again. "He's going to die if he keeps up what he's doing."

"Brooks, all you can do is encourage him to do what's healthy. You can't do it for him."

Brooks stared down the hall, at the nurses' desk, at the tile floor and the clinical surroundings. Then he looked Jazzy straight in the eye. "Will you marry me?"

Chapter Seven

Jazzy gazed at Brooks in stunned silence. Her heart was tripping so fast she could hardly breathe. Had he asked her to do what she thought he asked her to do? *Marry* him?

"Can you repeat that?" she asked haltingly.

He ran his hand down over his face, then looked at her as if maybe he should have kept his mouth shut. "I asked you to marry me. I know you think I'm absolutely crazy."

"No…" she started and didn't know quite how to finish or where to go from there. All she knew was, the idea of being married to Brooks Smith made her feel as if she was on top of a Ferris wheel, toppling over the highest point. "I just wanted you to repeat it so I know I wasn't hearing you wrong. You want to marry me?"

He took her hand in his and looked deep into her

eyes. "This isn't a joke, Jazzy. I'm not out of my mind. Really. But I need to solve this problem with my father. The only way he's going to let me in on the practice, the only way he's going to rest and stop wearing himself down, is if I'm really settled. I thought he was bluffing up to this point. I truly did. But he's not. Something is making him want this for me. A rival practice seems to have made the problem worse. So I can only see one solution. I have to give him what he wants."

"I don't understand," she said very quietly, his assessment not making her feel so tipsy anymore.

"He wants me to be married. Settled. So I need a wife. The way we've worked together the past week, I just know you'd be perfect."

"So you really *do* want me to marry you?"

"It wouldn't be a *real* marriage."

When he said those words, she found herself amazingly disappointed. How stupid was that?

He squeezed her hand and went on. "We would stay together for a year. In exchange, I'll deed over the land my grandmother left me. You can have the ranch you've always wanted, rescue horses, maybe even earn that business degree."

Suddenly Jazzy realized *she* was the one who must be crazy. She didn't want a ranch as much as she wanted a life with Brooks. She was falling for him, and she was falling *hard*. Working beside him for a year, living with him for a year, she'd be altogether gone. On the other hand, if they actually fell in love, maybe he'd change his mind about not wanting to stay married. On the other hand, if their relationship didn't work out, she'd have an out.

Living with Brooks, eating breakfast with him,

working in the office with him, spending evenings with him… What was she thinking?

"What would your grandmother think?"

"She would understand. She loved animals, too. And she'd be proud to watch you use it for good. She'd also understand I want Dad around as long as I can have him. Think about it, Jazzy. I'll show you the land. It's a great place for what you want to do. Imagine how long it would take you to save up to buy your own property."

"I don't even know if I could do it in ten years," she murmured.

"Exactly. We'd both be getting just what we need out of this deal."

The longer Jazzy looked into Brooks's eyes, the longer he told her all the reasons this would work, the more she believed him. She thought about his dad in that hospital bed and how this fake marriage could possibly set his mind at ease. Really, they'd be saving his life.

"Maybe you should think about this a little while," she said.

"I don't need to think about it. I'm not usually an impulsive person, but when I see the solution to a problem, then I take it. You're my solution, Jazzy. We can make this work. We like each other. We respect each other. We'd look at this as a partnership."

Yes, they would. It would be a bargain…a good deal. They'd each be getting something they needed. She'd definitely be moving her life forward.

"But didn't your dad say he wanted you to build a house on that land?"

"We'll have to take this piece by piece. I think he'll just be so overjoyed I'm getting married, that the house won't matter."

"But what happens at the end of the year? With your dad, I mean?"

"By then his health will be stabilized. He'll be on the road to healthier living. I'll be taking care of most of the work at the practice, maybe even bringing in a partner. We'll just tell him it didn't work out. We jumped in too soon. But that's not to think about now. Now, we just need to convince him we fell in love and this is exactly what we want."

"Will you keep the new office?"

"Yes, I think I would. Dad would feel as if he still had a say over what was going on at his place. Little by little, I'd handle the whole load."

"You'd be giving up a year of your life for your father. Is that what you really want to do?"

"Didn't we both say family is what matters most? A year of my life is nothing. I don't know how much longer I'll have him. I have to do this, Jazzy. Will you help me? Will you make it work?"

She thought about a wedding, a bridal gown, vows. She thought about the ranch and the horses that needed to be rescued and a life in Rust Creek Falls. She thought about being far enough away from her own family to have a life of her own without their meddling. This really could work.

And her and Brooks? Well, she'd just have to keep her growing feelings under wraps and pretend this was business all the way. But in the meantime, she'd enjoy every minute she was with him. How much of a hardship could that be?

"There *is* another big advantage in this for me," she confessed with a smile.

"What's that?"

"My family will be getting what they want. They want to see me married and settled down, too. Maybe they'll stop worrying about me, at least long enough that I can put my own life in the direction *I* plan without their interference."

He was still holding her hand and now he squeezed it gently. "So you'll do this? You'll marry me?"

Her heart felt fuller than it ever had before. "Yes, I'll marry you. What do we do first?"

Brooks stood beside Jazzy as they looked up at the pine-filled mountains, snow-capped peaks, the quiet serenity of the property his grandmother had left him. Was he absolutely crazy?

After his father's adamant refusal to do what was best for him, Brooks had known he had to do something drastic, really drastic. He'd asked himself what would settle his dad's mind most; what would provide the opportunity for him to change his health in the right direction? Brooks had realized only one thing would do that—his own marriage.

Of course he wouldn't ask just any woman to marry him. That would be truly stupid. But he knew Jazzy's background. He knew what she thought about her family. He knew she worked hard. He knew she had a goal, but wasn't sure how to get there. A marriage on paper for a year would suit both their purposes.

"What do you think?" he asked her.

They stood by his truck pulled helter-skelter over a rutted lane. This property, like his dad's clinic and ranch, was located on the higher end of town. There had been some erosion from the waters, but overall, it had survived quite nicely.

"How big is it?" Jazzy asked in a small voice, and he wondered if she was anxious or nervous about his proposal and her acceptance. Of course she was. They were stepping into untested waters.

"Ten acres."

"The property looks like it's never been touched by a man's hand."

"It hasn't. My grandmother's ranch, next door so to speak, was sold when she died. She'd subdivided this parcel for me, and I never knew that."

"Are you sure about this, Brooks? You really want to let this property go?"

"It's a pretty piece of land, Jazzy, and, yes, it was my grandmother's. But it's not as if I'd be selling it for a housing development. You want to do something worthwhile with it, and you deserve compensation for giving me a year of your life."

She gazed out over the hills and pine forests, rather than at him. "When do you want to get married?"

Was that a little tremble he heard in her voice? Was she as terrifically unsure about this idea as he was? Maybe so, but Brooks only knew how to do one thing—forge ahead.

"As soon as possible. In fact, the sooner, the better. As soon as we put Dad's mind to rest, the quicker he'll take it easy. I'm hoping we can get this planned and accomplished in a week to ten days."

"That's fast."

"Having third and fourth thoughts? You can back out."

Now she did turn toward him. What he saw in her big, blue eyes made his chest tighten and his throat practically close. She was vulnerable, maybe more vulnerable than he was. Maybe planning this wedding put an impediment in her road instead of clearing it. From what he'd heard, little girls had dreams of Prince Charming and happily-ever-after. He certainly wasn't offering her that. The good thing was, however, she'd be free and clear of him in a year. Then she could resume her search for Mr. Right and think about having babies.

The idea of Jazzy and babies didn't help that tight feeling in his chest. "This wouldn't be a real marriage, Jazzy. You'd have nothing to fear from me. We'll be... housemates."

That caused a crease in her brow. "Housemates," she repeated. Then after a huge breath, she asked, "Where would we get married?"

"Dad won't believe this is the real thing unless we get married in a church."

"I'll have to shop for a wedding dress."

"And we'll have to order a cake. I'm hoping we can use the church's social hall for a small reception."

"You've already planned all this out in your mind."

"Yes, I have, but all the details can be up to you. After all, it's your wedding."

"And yours," she said softly. "There is something I'd like to know before we move on with our plans."

"What?"

"Can you tell me why your fiancée broke her engagement to you?"

The wind sifted in the branches of the pine boughs and Brooks felt snow in the air. Not a big one yet. Maybe flurries tonight. He knew he was distracting himself with the idea of the weather because Jazzy's question turned the knife that sometimes still seemed to be stuck in his heart.

"Brooks?" Jazzy asked, looking up at him, expecting the truth and nothing but. Jazzy wasn't anything like Lynnette. Nothing at all. That was a terrifically good thing.

"There were several reasons. You want me to run down the list?"

"Brooks—"

He shook his head. "Even after all this time, it's still hard for me to talk about."

"Do you ever talk about it with anyone?"

His answer was quick and succinct. "No."

Instead of prompting, poking, or encouraging, Jazzy just stood there and waited, looking at him with those big blue eyes, her blond hair blowing in the breeze.

"We were at Colorado State together and engaged for a year. She was three years younger than I was and I didn't see that as a problem at first."

"At first?"

"She still liked to go out with her friends. Since I was buried in studies or practical vet experience most of the time, she went. I really didn't think anything of it. My parents had had a good marriage and I just expected the same thing to happen to me."

Jazzy's expression asked the question, *Why didn't it?* She didn't have to say the words. A nip in the air made his cheeks burn, or maybe it was just thinking about the whole thing all over again.

"She'd come home with me on holidays and vacations. When we were home, I helped Dad and she knew I expected to join his practice after I graduated."

"So you thought everything was on the table?"

"Yes, I did." He realized Jazzy was getting an inkling of what was coming next. "A few months before my

graduation, Lynnette started asking questions like—
Did I really want to practice in Rust Creek Falls? Did I
really want to live there all my life? I told her that was
my plan. I'd never been anything but honest about it. I
think the real turning point was a job offer I had from a
practice in Billings, and one in Denver. When I turned
them both down, she began acting differently. Or maybe
that had started even before that. I don't know."

He saw Jazzy take a little breath as if she guessed
what he was going to say.

"A month before I was scheduled to graduate, she
told me she'd fallen in love with someone else, someone else who wanted the same kind of life she did. She
didn't want to be married to someone who might work
eighteen-hour days, whose phone could beep anytime
with an emergency, whose small-town life was just too
limited for what she had planned."

"Oh, Brooks."

This was why he didn't talk about what happened.
This was expressly why he hadn't told Jazzy. He didn't
want her pity. He turned away from her to look in another direction, to escape the awkwardness, to bandage
up his pride all over again. He was looking up into the
sky for that snow when he felt a small hand on his arm.
It was more than a tap, almost like a gentle clasp. Her
touch was thawing icy walls that surrounded his heart,
had surrounded it for a long time.

"Brooks?" There was compassion in her voice and
he had to face it. That was the right thing to do. He
turned back to her.

"Thank you," she said simply. "For telling me. I understand a little better why—" She shook her head.
"Never mind. It helps me understand you."

"So you think you have to understand me to marry me?" he joked, trying to shake off the ghost of the past, trying to look forward.

"That would help, especially in front of your dad. If we're going to pretend we're madly in love and this was a whirlwind courtship, understanding each other goes a long way, don't you think?"

Madly in love...whirlwind courtship...pretending.

Just what were they getting themselves into?

"You're what?" Barrett asked, looking stupefied an hour later.

"We're getting married," Brooks said, with more determination than enthusiasm, Jazzy thought.

"Of course we'll wait until you're feeling better," Jazzy explained.

Barrett looked from one of them to the other, his eyes narrowing. "And just when did this romance start?"

"Jazzy's been here since July," Brooks answered off-handedly. Then he took her hand, moved his thumb over the top, and smiled at his dad, though Jazzy thought the smile was a little forced. She was aware of his big hand engulfing hers, of how close they were standing, of how her life was going to be connected to his.

Studying them again, their joined hands, the way they were leaning toward each other, she wondered exactly what he saw. After all, she and Brooks had developed a bond. They wanted the best for his father. They had their own goals. They believed this was a good way to achieve them. Besides all that, they genuinely liked each other. If she could just keep that liking under wraps, if she could just pretend Brooks was a good friend, not a man she was extremely attracted to, everything would be fine.

The flabbergasted expression left Barrett's face, but he still seemed wary. "You two have been spending a lot of time together, haven't you?"

"For more than a week, we've been together most hours in the day," Brooks supplied easily.

"Yes, I know. Setting up a *rival* practice."

"Dad, it doesn't have to be a rival practice."

Barrett took another look at their clasped hands. "We'll talk about that after this marriage takes place. Why is it you don't want a long engagement?"

"You and Mom didn't have a long engagement, did you?" Brooks countered.

Barrett looked surprised that Brooks remembered that.

"Mom used to tell me stories about when the two of you met." Brooks added, "Come to think of it, you had a whirlwind courtship yourself, didn't you?"

"So your mother told you about those days?"

"She did. She was visiting friends in Rust Creek Falls and went to a barn dance. You were there. She told me as soon as you do-si-doed with her, she knew you were the one."

A shadow seemed to cross Barrett's face and Jazzy wondered if he was in pain. But the monitors were all steady. He was silent for a few moments and then said, "Those years were the happiest of my life. She was right. We both knew that night. So maybe...so maybe this sudden engagement of yours is in the genes. Maybe waiting is stupid when life is short."

"But you're going to have a long life, as soon as you change some of your ways," Brooks suggested.

"No one knows how long they have," Barrett said thoughtfully. "I'm going home tomorrow if some blasted machine doesn't beep the wrong thing."

"Are you sure you're ready to go home?" Jazzy asked.

"You know hospitals and insurance these days. I'm sure the doc wouldn't let me go home if he didn't think I could."

"You're not going home alone. I'll stay with you," Brooks concluded.

"There's no need for that."

"Dad, I insist. Even if it's just for a few days...to make sure you're back on your feet. Our practice isn't that busy yet and I can help out with yours. You've got to start taking care of yourself, and this is one best way of doing it."

Barrett assessed the two of them for a long time, then finally he addressed Jazzy. "I heard some of the volunteers are staying at Strickland's. Is that where you are?"

"Yes, sir, it is."

"Then let me propose a bargain. I'll let Brooks come and stay with me if you come and stay, too. I want to get to know my daughter-in-law-to-be."

Jazzy fought going into a panic. Staying with Barrett wasn't all that far-fetched. The problem was, she and Brooks would be under his eagle eye. They'd have to watch themselves every minute they were together. They'd have to watch every word they said, and really, truly act like a couple who'd fallen in love. She wouldn't look at Brooks because that could be a dead giveaway that there was a problem.

Instead, she focused on his dad. "That is an option, Mr. Smith. I'd like to get to know you better, too. But

I do think Brooks and I should discuss it before we decide."

Barrett didn't look at all upset with her suggestion. In fact, he waved his hand at the two of them to go outside the door. "So discuss! Then come back in here and tell me what you decided." He studied Brooks. "I think you chose a gal with a practical head on her shoulders. Go on now. Talk this out."

In the hall, Brooks pushed his hair back over his forehead and his eyebrows rose. "I can't expect you to stay at Dad's with me."

She was quiet a moment but then she decided, "Maybe it's for the best. We have a wedding to plan, and your dad needs somebody to keep on eye on him while you're at work. I can do that."

"Are you sure you don't want to back out of this whole venture? Dealing with two Smiths in close quarters might be too much to ask."

She thought about the horse-rescue ranch she wanted to manage. She thought about Brooks's dad and his health. She thought about staying at his dad's ranch with Brooks. Did she really want to do this?

Her answer came easily and freely. "We'll plan a small, quiet wedding, and we'll take care of your dad. It will be a piece of cake."

A piece of cake, Brooks thought wryly the next day as he handed his father his remote and made sure he was settled in his recliner. "Is there anything you need? A glass of water? Something to eat? Jazzy and I went shopping last night in Kalispell and the refrigerator is stocked with good stuff."

"Rabbit food, probably," Barrett grumbled. "You know I don't like rabbit food."

"I have a copy of the diet the doctor recommended."

"Fine. I'll eat what you want when you're here. But as soon as you two leave—"

Brooks stepped in front of his father's chair and stared him down. "I lost Mom. I don't want to lose you. So try to cooperate a little, all right?"

Barrett was about to answer when Jazzy came into the room with a tray. On it, Brooks saw a turkey sandwich, a salad and a dish of fruit. He didn't know what his dad was going to say about that.

Jazzy glanced around the living room. "This is nice. Homey. This is where you raised Brooks?"

If his father had been about to argue with Brooks, he seemed to have changed his mind. "Yeah, it is. He was born here, in the downstairs bedroom, in the four-poster bed." Barrett waved his hand toward the hall in the back of the house.

"Really? A home birth? Was that planned or an accident?"

"It was in the middle of a snowstorm is what it was," Barrett elaborated. "My mom happened to be here so I didn't have to handle it myself. He came out squalling."

Jazzy set the tray on the table next to his father. "I hope you like this. The turkey is supposed to be the deli's oven-baked kind. The salad is something I cooked up. It's my own dressing. And the fruit—I hope you like apples and strawberries."

To Brooks's surprise, his father looked up at Jazzy and smiled. "It looks great and I think my stomach just growled. Good timing."

Brooks felt like shaking his head and rolling his eyes but he knew better.

"I'm going to make soup tonight if you're okay with that. My mom's vegetable soup can make anybody feel better about anything."

"So you know how to cook?" Barrett asked with a wink, taking a big bite of his sandwich.

"I'm not a wonderful cook, but I can make anything basic. And I can always call my mother to find out what I don't know."

"Did you tell your family about the wedding yet?"

Jazzy's face was serious for a moment then lightened. "Not yet. That's on my list of things to do today."

"I have a couple of Dad's outside calls to make, but then I'll be at the clinic for a few appointments this afternoon," Brooks informed them both.

Barrett scowled. "You think you'll be able to handle that on your own with Jazzy here? I'm really fine alone."

"You're not going to be alone, Dad, not for the next few days. So just get used to that idea. Jazzy, if you need me, or he becomes too bullheaded, call me. I put your suitcase in the upstairs bedroom, the one with the yellow rose-print wallpaper." To his father, Brooks said, "I want to talk to Jazzy about some wedding details. Will you be okay for a few minutes?"

"I'll be fine." His father pressed a button on the remote. "Don't worry about me."

Brooks crooked his finger at Jazzy and they went into the kitchen. She wore khakis today with a red blouse and looked like a million bucks. He'd been trying not to notice but that was hard with her blond hair swishing over her shoulder as she moved, her blue eyes flashing up at him, her smile curling like an old, forgotten song around him. There was something about Jazzy that was starting to make him ache. That was the dumbest thought he'd ever had.

"You want to talk about the wedding?" she asked.

"I called the courthouse this morning and all we have to do is go in and get the license and we're good. I also checked with the church and we can have the service next Wednesday. Is that all right with you?"

"If you think your dad will be okay by then."

"Not okay, but I have the feeling we'll have to tie him down long before then. He listens to you much better than he listens to me. So anything we want him to do is better coming from you. Do you think you can handle that?"

"I'm used to dealing with a younger brother. I can handle it."

Brooks chuckled, and then he looked at her and he wanted to kiss her. No way, but yes, that was definitely what was on his mind.

To change gears and to drive in a different direction away from that train of thought, he asked, "So you're going to call your family later?"

"I suppose I'll have to now. Your dad's bound to ask me about it."

"Do you want to wait until I'm around to do it?"

"No. I'll call Mom and she'll spread the word. Everyone else will probably call me. I might have to turn off my phone for the next few days. What bothers me most is that I can't be completely honest with them, at least not yet."

"It's not too late to back out."

She looked as if she wanted to say something about that, but she bit her lip and didn't.

With that gesture that was both innocent and sexy, he couldn't keep himself from reaching out and pushing her silky blond hair behind her ear. "We're in this together and it will work out."

She turned her cheek into his palm and they stood there that way...in silence. Finally she was the one who straightened and leaned away from his hand. "You'd better get to work. Covering two practices yourself isn't going to be easy."

"At least mine's just getting started. I'll manage. I forgot to tell you with bringing Dad home and all, the Kalispell practice found another vet who's relocating from Bozeman. So now I can focus here."

"That's wonderful news." Jazzy threw her arms around his neck and gave him a hug. "I'm so glad. I was worried about you spreading yourself too thin."

All of his senses registered her sweet smell, her soft skin, her genuine hug. On top of that, he realized he couldn't remember when a woman had last worried about him. That aching took up residence in his chest again. He pushed it away as he leaned away from her.

Taking his jacket from the back of the kitchen chair, he shrugged into it. He felt her watching him as he walked to the door.

"I'm just a phone call away," he reminded her, meaning it.

As Jazzy gave him an unsure smile, he wished he was staying right there in that kitchen with her. That thought drove him out of his childhood home. It drove him to concentrate on where he was going and the animals he'd be treating. It drove him to think about *anything* but Jazzy.

Chapter Eight

"Mom, take it easy, I know what I'm doing."

Jazzy glanced in the living room and down the hall to the first-floor bedroom. Brooks was in there with his dad setting up a baby monitor he'd bought so he'd be able to hear his father if he needed anything. She really didn't want either of them to overhear this conversation.

"How can I take it easy when you broke up with someone recently, and now you're getting married?" her mother asked.

"Griff and I were never right. You and Dad, Abby and Laila and Annabel liked him. Jordyn and Brody liked him, too, but they understood better how I felt."

"And how did you feel?"

"Like all of you were rooting for a relationship I didn't want. When Laila told me she knew Griff was going to propose, I had to break it off."

Her mother sighed. "Griff was such a good catch."

"Mom—"

"How can you be getting married when you haven't known this man very long? What's his name again?"

"It's Brooks Smith. I told you. He's a veterinarian."

"That's about *all* you've told me. You didn't even tell us you were dating him. Dean didn't even mention it."

"Dean doesn't know everything," Jazzy said, holding on to her temper.

"So is this going to be a long engagement?"

Jazzy swallowed. This was the hard part. "No, we're getting married in a week to ten days. I don't have the details yet. As soon as I do, I'll let you know. But Mom, I know this is quick, so it's really not necessary for all of you to come. Really. But if you do, I can reserve rooms at a Kalispell motel."

"A week to ten days! Jazzy. Why the rush? You're not—"

"No, I'm not pregnant. This is just…right. Brooks and I know it." Jazzy was realizing more and more that this marriage *would* be right for her. How Brooks might feel at the end of the year was another matter.

"I wish your father was here." Her mom had mentioned that her father had gone to visit a friend.

"Dad won't change my mind."

"Then maybe your sisters can."

Jazzy knew she was going to have to say what she didn't want to say. However, maybe it was time. "Mom, do you know why I left Thunder Canyon?"

"Yes. You went to Rust Creek Falls to help the flood victims."

"That's true. But I also needed to get away from all of you. I needed to find out who I am on my own without four sisters' opinions, and Brody telling me what he thinks is best, too. I needed to make up my own mind about everything from work to getting a degree to dating."

Her mother was silent for a few moments and Jazzy was afraid she'd hurt her. But then she said, "You never told us any of this."

"I don't think I fully understood what was happening until I was here. I mean, I knew I wanted to get away from something, but I wasn't exactly sure what it was. After I was here, I realized there's so much noise in our family, and its growing in leaps and bounds with Laila, Abby and Annabel finding their dream husbands. I felt lost sometimes. I felt invisible sometimes."

"Oh, Jazzy." Her mother's voice was filled with the compassion she felt for her.

"I don't feel that way here," she murmured. "I don't feel that way anymore. I feel like Brooks needs me—with work, and personal things, too. I feel like an equal…a partner."

Again, her mother went quiet. Finally she asked, "Jazzy, is this truly what you want?"

"It *is*. And as soon as I know more about what's happening, I'll let you know. I promise."

"Your sisters are going to call you."

"I know."

"Brody might, too."

"I know."

"And you won't get upset with them because they care."

"I won't. But you might as well tell them my mind is made up. I'm getting married to Brooks Smith."

After the conversation was over and Jazzy had ended

the call, she felt worn out. This afternoon, she'd made soup and generally checked on Barrett, yet she'd also had to dodge *his* questions about her relationship with Brooks. She'd sidetracked him with anecdotes about her brother and sisters and her family. She'd done pretty well, but she didn't know how long she could keep it up.

At least Barrett was turning in now, and she and Brooks wouldn't have to deal with his scrutiny as they had during dinner and a few games of gin rummy.

She went down the hall to Barrett's room and found Brooks plugging the small monitor into a receptacle.

"So you're going to hear me snore all night?" Barrett was asking his son.

"I'm sure you don't snore all night. I'll sleep a lot better hearing you snore than I would worrying about the fact that you could need something."

Barrett gave a harrumph and turned to Jazzy. "So you called your parents?"

"I spoke with Mom. Dad wasn't there."

"And—"

Jazzy felt her cheeks getting a little hot. "They're concerned, of course, because it's short notice. But my mom just wants me to be happy." She went over to Brooks, took his hand and looked up at him adoringly, though it really wasn't much of an act to do that.

This is what they'd been doing all evening, and he played along with her, too. Leaning toward her, he wrapped his arm around her shoulders. "They'll come around. I can't wait to meet them."

Something in his eyes told her that he was being honest about that. Did he want to meet them to learn more about her? Or because he'd be dealing with them, maybe, for the next year? This was all getting a bit confusing. Boundaries were blurring. Were they colleagues or were they friends?

Taking his arm from around her, Brooks said, "You're all set up, Dad. You don't have to do a thing. Just leave it on, and if you need anything, yell."

"If I yell, you'll hear me without the monitor."

Jazzy had to smile at that.

"So you two are turning in, too?" Barrett asked with a quirked brow, as if he wondered if they'd be sleeping in separate rooms.

"I have a few journal articles to catch up on," Brooks said.

"I'll turn in early because I want to get up and make both of you breakfast," Jazzy added.

"We're both early risers," Barrett warned her.

"No problem there. I am, too. We'll see you in the morning."

But before she and Brooks exited the room, Barrett called after her, "That was a fine right soup. I'm glad there's leftovers for tomorrow."

Jazzy laughed as she and Brooks entered the living room and headed for the staircase. They climbed it in silence.

After Brooks walked her to the guest-room door, he frowned. "I didn't think being around him was going to be so tough."

"That's because we're pretending."

They stared at each other, each weighing the other's motives, needs and ultimate goals. After what Brooks had told her, she understood now why he was a confirmed bachelor. He'd been hurt badly. As far as she knew, he'd never trust another woman. Yet there was something in the way he looked at her that told her he wasn't immune to her as a woman, and she knew there was something in the way she looked at him that told him he was a very attractive man.

"We're going to have to do a lot of pretending with my family, too," Jazzy warned him. "They're probably all going to call me. I told Mom I don't expect them to all make it to the wedding. After all, Annabel's husband is a doctor."

"So from what you've said, there's Abby and Cade, Laila and Jackson, Annabel and Thomas. Brody and Jordyn are still single."

"That's right. I told Mom I could reserve rooms at a Kalispell motel if they want to come up and stay overnight."

"That's probably a good idea."

"How many guests do you think we'll have?"

"Maybe about fifty."

With Brooks's eyes on hers, with him close and the memory of his arm around her still fresh, she said, "So we're really going to do this."

"We really are." He changed the subject before either of them thought too much about it. "Dad wants to help with chores tomorrow morning, but I told him that's out of the question."

"I can help."

"You're making breakfast."

"Breakfast takes about five minutes. I help with chores at home, you know."

He grinned at her. "You do, do you?"

"I'm not a city girl. I'm used to small-town Montana." Maybe she'd said it because she wanted to make the distinction between herself and Lynnette.

Brooks's eyes narrowed. "Are you trying to tell me something?"

"I'm trying to tell you, you can trust me to keep my word. You can trust me to be a partner in this. Helping you look after your dad means taking a load off your shoulders. I'll do that with you, Brooks. After all, it's our agreement."

Even without the agreement she would do it for him if he asked.

Brooks was close, but now he moved a little closer. The nerve in his jaw jumped and his eyes darkened. She thought she knew what that darkening meant. It was his desire. He was fighting it for all he was worth, and she had been fighting hers, too. But now, she didn't know what was more prudent. She wished he'd act on that desire.

As he leaned closer to her, she thought he might.

But he didn't even touch her this time. His lips, that had been so sensual moments before, thinned and drew into a tight line. His shoulders squared and his spine became even straighter.

Then he let out a breath and he shook his head. "I confided in you about Lynnette, but that's not something I do very often. And even though I did, trusting is tough for me."

Although he hadn't touched her, she had to touch him. She clasped his arm. "Brooks, I will help you with your dad. That's the point of all this, isn't it?"

"Yes, it is."

She had the feeling that when he said the words, he was reminding them both of the reason for their marriage. He didn't want either of them to forget it.

* * *

In the barn the following morning, Brooks made sure he concentrated on the chores and not on Jazzy. That was hard, though. Her soft voice got under his skin as she talked to the horses. It was tough not to watch her jeans pull across her backside as she carried feed to the stalls. While he replaced water buckets, he remembered the meal she'd cooked last night, the way the house had smelled so good, the fresh-baked biscuits that had fallen apart when he'd broken them. He found himself easily imagining coming home to her every night.

"Are you going to play gin rummy all day today with Dad?" he asked from across the stall.

"Not *all* day. If you need me to work on anything for the office, I can do it here. Just let me know. I want to cook and freeze dinners so your dad can just pull them out when he needs them."

"There *are* frozen dinners."

"There are. But they have preservatives, and maybe not as tight a watch on calories, fat, all that. I found some good recipes online."

"You're going above and beyond the call of duty."

"If I sit with your dad and talk with him, it's hard to deflect some of his questions. He watches the two of us like a hawk. At least if I'm busy, he can't ask me about…us."

Brooks knew staying here was hard for Jazzy, too, and he shouldn't take his frustration out on her. "Tonight, instead of talking and playing gin, we'll make out the guest list. You can bet he'll have opinions on that. We should also decide on food. The women in the church's social club can provide a down-home meal with fried chicken if we'd like that. After all, your family is traveling all the way from Thunder Canyon. A hot meal would be good."

"That would be nice," she agreed. She studied him for a few moments, then commented, "You were awful quiet this morning while we were doing chores. Are you worried about the wedding?"

He wasn't worried about the wedding. He was concerned about what came after and the attraction he was beginning to feel toward Jazzy that he didn't understand and couldn't deflect.

"The wedding should pretty much plan itself. When are you going to get a dress?"

"I found one online. It should be here soon."

"Won't your mom and sisters be disappointed you chose a dress without them?"

"I don't want to spend too much time around them right now, Brooks, for the same reason I don't want to sit and talk with your dad. They'll understand I have to do this on short notice."

But he saw the look in Jazzy's eyes and knew she wasn't convinced of that. Were they making a mess of their lives? He knew this was right to do for him, but Jazzy? She was the kind of girl who still had stars in her eyes, who dreamed of bridal veils and babies. He'd bet on it.

For that reason, he thought about another errand he should run. He really should buy Jazzy a wedding present, just something small to tell her he appreciated what she was doing. He didn't know if Crawford's General Store would have anything, but they might. Nina ordered some unique gifts simply because Rust Creek Falls inhabitants didn't always want to travel to

Kalispell to find what they needed. He'd stop in there sometime today because things were only going to get more hectic before the wedding.

"Is there anything I should know about the horses? Should I come out to check on them during the day?" Jazzy asked as she stroked a gray's nose.

"No, I'll let them out into the pasture before I'm done here. Why don't you go on up and start Dad's breakfast."

"Trying to get rid of me?" she asked teasingly.

Yes, he was. But he couldn't tell her that. When he didn't answer right away, she asked, "Brooks?"

"Once Dad's up, he doesn't like to wait around for breakfast. I don't want him coming out here and thinking he can help. Maybe you can head him off at the pass."

"I'll do that."

When she swished by him, he almost reached out and pulled her into his arms. But he didn't.

At the doorway to the barn, she stopped. "Sunnyside up eggs, or scrambled?"

"Any way you want to make them."

She flashed him a smile and was gone.

Brooks groaned and picked up a pitchfork.

A wedding present for Jazzy.

Brooks strode through Crawford's, not knowing what he was looking for, just hoping that when he saw it, it would be right. He was hoping he could find that one special thing that he knew she'd like. Jewelry was always the best bet, but thinking about it, he hadn't seen Jazzy wearing much jewelry. Of course she wouldn't to work with animals or painting or helping with construction at the new elementary school.

Pearls were a traditional wedding gift. His dad had given his mom pearls. In fact, he knew they were still kept in his dad's safe. But this wasn't going to be a traditional wedding. It wasn't going to be a real marriage, so traditional didn't work.

He glanced at vases and candy and even boots. He spotted sparkly earrings and a necklace that would have hung practically to her navel. But then his gaze fell on the right thing, the perfect thing, something that was necessary yet something that could be a little fashionable, too. The Montana Silversmith's watch. His gaze targeted the rectangular-faced one with the black leather band and the scrollwork in silver and gold that made the band fancy.

When he saw who was behind the counter today, he smiled. It was Nina Crawford. She was looking as pretty and fit as usual, yet when his gaze ran down over the front of her, even in the oversize T-shirt, he could see the small bump.

"Nina, it's good to see you."

She frowned and laid her hand on her tummy. "It's good to see you, too, Brooks. I guess you noticed." She leaned close to him and whispered, "I just started showing, almost overnight."

"That's the way it happens sometimes. At least that's what I've heard." Though he did wonder who the father was.

Nina asked, "How can I help you?"

"Can I see that watch?" It was inside the case.

"That's a woman's watch."

"Yes, I know."

"Are you dating someone?" She sounded surprised and he knew why. Most everyone in town knew he'd said more than once, he'd never get married. But never say never.

"I'm not just dating someone. I'm going to marry someone."

"Why, Brooks Smith! Who's the lucky girl?"

"Jazzy Cates."

"One of those volunteers from Thunder Canyon?"

"That's right. She's been helping out here since after the flood. I thought this would be a nice wedding present."

"It's a *beautiful* wedding present. Any woman would love to have it." She stood back and eyed him again. "I just can't believe you're getting married. Did the flood change the way you look at life? It did for many folks around here."

He couldn't say it did, really, though Jazzy had maintained it had changed her outlook some. "Not so much. I guess I'm just feeling it's time to put down roots and forget about the past."

"That's not so easy to do," Nina said. "Take the mayoral election for instance. Collin Traub versus my brother. In the past, there was a family feud between the Traubs and Crawfords that no one even remembers anymore. But the bad feelings are still there. Who are you voting for?"

"Collin did a good job after the flood, bringing everyone together."

"You're kidding, right?"

"No, I'm not. I saw him in action."

Nina crossed her arms over her chest, "And my brother didn't do a good job?"

Now he'd set his foot in it. "It's going to require some thought, but I think my vote's going to be for Collin."

"I should charge you extra for the watch."

"But you won't."

She gave him a wry smile. "No, I won't. Do you want it gift wrapped?"

"You do that here?"

"Sure do. I have a pretty gold foil that should do the trick, if you have time to wait."

"I have a few minutes. Thanks, Nina. I really appreciate it."

"I don't need you here," Barrett said for about the tenth time.

Jazzy and Brooks exchanged a look across the kitchen table.

Barrett motioned to the papers Jazzy had spread across the table—pictures of wedding cakes and flowers, a list of guests and a to-do list that ran on for two pages. "You have lots to do and not much time to do it in. And you can turn off that damn monitor, too," he told Brooks. "After tonight, I'm on my own. You have better things to do than babysitting."

Brooks wasn't sure he was ready to leave just yet. But he also didn't want his dad's blood pressure going up every time he thought about them being there. "I'll make you a deal."

"Uh-oh. Sounds like I'm going to get the short end of the stick again."

Jazzy laughed and Brooks realized the sound broke the tension. She seemed to be able to do that easily.

"Jazzy and I will leave, but I come out here to help you with the chores first thing in the morning and at the end of the day. And she stops in at lunch to make sure you're eating properly."

Barrett narrowed his eyes. "I don't mind seeing her pretty face at lunch, and I'll take your help with the chores in the morning. But I'm on my own after that."

"Dad—"

"Don't give me that tone of voice, son. You want to help out with the animals, fine. You want to help out at the clinic, fine. But then I need my private time."

"Another condition, then. You get one of those new smartphones so we can talk face-to-face."

"I don't need—"

"Mr. Smith, I think you need to put Brooks's mind at rest. He won't be able to work if he's worried about you. Is a new phone such a bad thing?"

Barrett sighed. "You two aren't going to give up, are you?" After a lengthy pause, he decided, "All right, a new phone, Brooks helping out with the animals and with the practice, and you keeping me company at lunch. But don't think that's going to go on forever, either."

"We'd never think that," they said in unison, and then they both laughed.

Barrett shook his head. "You're even beginning to sound like a married couple. So did you set the date?"

"I talked with the reverend tonight," Brooks said. "Next Wednesday evening. Jazzy and I are going to the social hall tomorrow to check things out."

"I'm paying for the reception," Barrett said.

Brooks looked at him, surprised. "You don't have to do that."

"That's not a matter of *have to*. I want to. It's the least I could do for all you're doing for me. Why don't you two go take a last check of the barn, so I can watch my TV in peace."

This time, Brooks didn't argue with his father. He hadn't seen Jazzy all day, and he'd missed her. It was an odd feeling, one he couldn't remember having even with Lynnette.

"I'll grab my jacket," Jazzy said and did just that. She pushed all the papers into a pile and slipped them into a folder.

Once they were outside and walking toward the barn, she said, "I think your dad wants some peace and quiet."

"He's used to living alone. I can see why having us around is tough."

"So which cake did you like?" she asked him. "The one with the little pedestal, the layer cake with the flowers in pink and yellow around the border, or the all-white cake with a dove sitting at the edge of each layer? Melba said she can do any of them. She's a terrific baker and offered to do it when I told her we were getting married."

"It really doesn't matter to me, Jazzy. Just choose one. Any one will be all right, as long as the cake's good." He could see that wasn't what she wanted to hear. She wanted him to be enthusiastic. But he was having trouble with enthusiasm for this wedding when it was going to be fake. Certainly he didn't want more than that, did he?

She stopped him with her hand on his arm. "You really don't care?"

The night had turned cool and very damp. Suddenly snow flurries began floating around them. "It's not that I don't care, Jazzy. I want you to have what you want. Doves or pedestals don't make a difference to me. But if they do to you, pick the one that makes you happy."

She gazed up at him, and in the glow of the barn's floodlight, he could see she looked confused.

"So it's not that you don't care, you're just not particular."

"That's the gist of it. Though I do prefer chocolate cake to something…exotic."

"Like white?" she teased.

He took her by the shoulders and gave her a gentle little shake. Her hair fell over his hand, turning him on. When Jazzy was around these days, he got way too revved up. Maybe he should keep his distance from her until the wedding. That wasn't going to be so hard unless…

He had something to ask her…to invite her to do. "We're getting married next week." If he said it often enough, he might believe it.

"I know," she said softly.

At that very moment, kissing her was the top thing on his to-do list. But he had to cross it off. "When we leave Dad's, you'll be going back to Strickland's till the wedding. But when we move in together…I just want you to know you can trust me. I have two bedrooms and you'll have your privacy in yours."

"I wasn't worried about—" She stopped and looked him straight in the eyes. "I trust you."

She trusted him. That was a vote of confidence he had to live up to.

"Are we eventually going to move to Rust Creek Falls?" she asked.

He'd been giving that some thought. "That makes sense, too. Since the Kalispell practice found someone to replace me, there's no need for me to stay there.

After we're married, we'll look around and see what's available."

"It sounds like a plan."

The snow was coming down a little heavier now, and Jazzy raised her face to it. A few flakes landed on her eyelashes—pretty, long, blond eyelashes. She opened her mouth and caught a few flakes on her tongue, giving him a grin.

His stomach clenched, his body tightened and he knew his plan to keep his distance would go along just fine as long as he didn't kiss her.

Chapter Nine

Jazzy stood in the social hall of the church the following evening, still not quite believing she was planning her wedding.

Her wedding.

She'd never thought it would be like this. Her chest tightened and her eyes grew misty.

Standing beside her, Brooks must have realized her emotions were getting the best of her because he asked, "Is something wrong?"

"Not really," she said, her voice betraying her.

He lifted her chin, and his touch excited her as it always did. "What is it?" he asked gently.

She summed it all up the only way she could. "It's our wedding day. I never thought it would be like this—just something to plan and get through."

He studied her for a very long time.

Then he asked, "Do you have that CD you burned at the office today of your favorite songs?"

"Yes," she said warily, glancing toward her purse that was sitting on one of the tables.

"Hold on a minute. I'll be right back."

When he started to stride away, she clasped his arm. "Where are you going? We really should get back to your dad." They would be moving out this weekend. She'd be going back to Strickland's until they married and Brooks would be staying at his condo once more.

"If we're leaving him on his own this weekend, we have to trust him to behave. But I asked Charlie to make an unexpected visit after we left tonight. They're probably deep into a discussion about what teams are going to make it to the Super Bowl this year."

When he turned away from her again, she asked, "But where are you going?"

"Patience, Jazzy. I'll be right back."

Men said they didn't understand women. That was definitely a two-way street.

For a few minutes, Jazzy believed Brooks had deserted her. Maybe that's what she expected. In the end, wasn't this kind of marriage all about that? Leaving each other with no strings? Unfortunately for her, she was going to have strings.

She wandered about the hall, thinking about flowers for the tables. Maybe white mums…

Brooks reappeared. He ordered, "Give me the CD."

She did and he went to a little door mounted on the wall and inserted a small key. He opened it, manipulated whatever was inside, and came back to her without the CD. Moments later, her music began playing and he opened his arms to her. "Okay, let's take a spin and see how it feels."

Was he serious? She felt a little ridiculous.

"Come on, Jazzy. Let's do more than plan. Let's practice our first dance."

When she still hesitated, he offered, "Look, I can understand you don't want me to treat our wedding as if it's just an appointment on the calendar. I'm not. Let's dance."

She felt a bit foolish now. After all, their wedding *was* an appointment on the calendar. It wasn't a *real* wedding. That fact made her so deeply sad.

Gratefully, Brooks didn't see her underlying confusion because he went on, "I think we've been trying to avoid the pretense of the whole thing. You hate deceiving Dad as much as I do. We just have to keep remembering the greater good."

So that's what he thought they were both doing, pretending for the greater good. *She* wasn't pretending. As world-shaking as it was, she'd fallen in love with Brooks Smith! Who knew that could happen in these strange circumstances? All she knew was that she never felt this way with Griff or anyone else, for that matter. She was an experienced dater. Truth be told, she hadn't even gone on anything resembling a date with Brooks. But each time they were together, it felt like a date. Each time they were together, she was sinking deeper into a whirl of emotion—and she wasn't sure how she'd ever pull herself out.

Gosh, she should write a country song.

Stepping closer to Brooks, she let him take her into his arms. His clasp was loose at first as the music swirled around them. As she gazed up into his eyes, however, his hold tightened a bit and then a bit more. She liked the feel of his strong arms around her. She liked the feel of the softness of his T-shirt against her cheek. He was so…so…male and she felt as if she were drowning in that…drowning in him.

She had to distract herself before she started weaving dreams that would never come true. "Do you really believe your dad will be okay if we leave?"

"He's not giving us any choice. I found someone to help him with chores morning *and* evening. He's the son of one of Dad's neighbors. And I'm going to insist Dad keep his cell phone on him at all times. I'll be at his practice during the day if I'm not out on call, so I can check on him between patients. With Charlie checking, too, all the bases will be covered."

All the bases except home base…her heart.

"I really want to rent a place in Rust Creek Falls so we're closer to Dad," Brooks continued. "But I checked with the real-estate agent. Since the flood, a nice place is hard to find. My condo in Kalispell will have to do until something becomes available. In fact, why don't we take a drive there when we're finished here?"

Touring the condo where Brooks lived would tell her even more about him. "Sure."

Suddenly Brooks released her, but he didn't go far. He reached into the pocket of his jeans. "Before I forget." He withdrew a chain with two keys. "There's a key to my place, and a key to Dad's."

She held them in her palm and the reality of living with Brooks shook her a little. She pocketed the keys. "Thank you."

"You're welcome." Taking her in his arms again, he brought her closer.

She'd watched couples dancing on TV. She'd danced with a few of her dates, too. But the pleasure of dancing with Brooks surpassed anything she'd watched or anything she'd ever felt. Now that they were pressed even closer together, she let his thighs guide hers. She let her cheek actually rest against his shirt. She could feel him breathing.

Although she fought against it, a happily-ever-after dream began to take shape and there was nothing she could do about it.

On Friday, Jazzy slipped Brooks's key into his door lock and opened the door. Then she waved to Cecilia who gave her a thumbs-up sign and drove away.

Everything seemed under control in Barrett's clinic, and Brooks was going to be out on calls all day. There hadn't been any appointments at the Buckskin Clinic. For now, any emergencies that came in there were being forwarded to his dad's place, anyway. So Jazzy had told Brooks, barring any unforeseen circumstances, Cecilia would drive her to his place and she could make them dinner. His father seemed to crave more privacy and independence now that he was feeling better, and Brooks had liked the idea.

She picked up the bags she'd rested on the porch while she was opening the door and went inside. It was one floor with two bedrooms, a spacious living room, a small dining area, and a basic kitchen. It was obvious he didn't spend much time here. There wasn't a loose sneaker or a stray newspaper or magazine anywhere. The kitchen looked pristine, as if he never cooked in it. Most of all, she admired the floor-to-ceiling fireplace. She could imagine being curled up on the tan corduroy sofa that sat opposite, sharing a cozy evening with Brooks. Maybe more than a cozy evening.

Thoughts like those were invading her waking as well as sleeping hours now, and she wasn't pushing them away quite as forcefully. After all, love made you think about all aspects of being together. She now knew exactly what had caused those looks on Laila, Abby and Annabel's faces when they'd been falling in love.

Whenever Brooks entered her mind, she had to smile. Whenever she thought about him caring for an animal, her heart warmed. Whenever he got close, her stomach fluttered. All signs she'd never had before. Now she knew what they all added up to—love. This marriage wasn't going to be one of convenience for her. She was going to mean those vows when she said them. And Brooks...well, maybe a year would make a difference. Maybe, in their time together, he'd tumble head over heels in love with her, too.

She planned supper for around six-thirty. The time had seemed reasonable. After all, a pot roast could cook a little longer if Brooks was late. She'd wrapped baking potatoes in foil before popping them in the oven. Blueberry cobbler would stay warm for a while or could be reheated in the microwave. But at seven-thirty, she was still telling herself all that as she worried in earnest. At eight o'clock she got the call.

"Are you all right?" She tried to keep the note of panic from her voice.

"I'm fine. There was a break in fencing at one of the ranches and some calves got wound up in barbed wire. I ended up working by flashlight and I didn't have a cell signal to call sooner. Sorry about that."

"It's okay. I'll have dinner ready for you when you get home."

"It's probably ruined."

"Nope. The meat might be a little stringy, but it's salvageable. What's your ETA?"

"About fifteen minutes."

"Sounds good. See you then."

Jazzy hung up the phone, relieved that Brooks was okay. More than relieved, really.

Fifteen minutes to the dot later, she heard the garage door go up. She heard the door open into the mudroom. When Brooks appeared in the kitchen, she couldn't help but gasp. He was practically covered in mud!

"I haven't been calf-roping, but close to it," he joked.

He unbuttoned his jacket and shrugged out of it. It was wet as well as muddy, and he didn't know where to lay it.

She took it from him and plopped it in the mudroom sink. "I can get clothes from your room if you don't mind me opening your closet or drawers."

"I don't mind. I don't want to track mud in there. Second long drawer in the dresser. Just grab sweatpants and a sweatshirt."

Hurrying off to his room, she switched on the light and looked around. There was a four-poster, king-size bed, a dresser with a detached mirror, a chest of drawers by the closet and a caned-back chair next to the bed. His bedspread was imprinted with mountains and moose, and the blinds were navy like the background of the spread. This was a thoroughly masculine room, and when she thought about that bed and him in it—

Quickly she went to the dresser and pulled out pants and a shirt, then hurried back to the mudroom. He'd shut the door. She could hear the spigot from the sink running, so she knocked.

"I'm washing off," he said. "Just drop them on the other side of the door and I'll grab them."

After they were married, would she be able to open that door and just walk in? Would he want her to?

Crossing to the kitchen, she pulled the food from the oven and arranged their plates. The vegetables had practically disintegrated, but the meat was surely tender. She fixed two plates, but instead of arranging them on the table, she took them into the living room and set them on the coffee table.

When Brooks came into the living room, he looked like a different person from the mud-splattered one who'd come home.

"Soap and water make a difference," she teased.

"Soap and water might not make a difference for those clothes."

"That's why man invented washing machines. You'd be amazed."

He glanced at the meal on the coffee table. "I already am."

She patted the sofa next to her. "Come on. I bet you're cold. It's supposed to go down to freezing out there tonight. A hot meal will help you warm up again."

He smiled and sat on the sofa beside her. That butterfly feeling in her stomach wasn't because of hunger.

They ate side by side. Jazzy was aware of every bite Brooks took, each sideways glance, the lift of his smile that said he approved of her cooking. She finished before he did, and she went to the kitchen for the whipped cream and cobbler.

After Brooks laid his head back against the sofa

cushion for a moment, he eyed her soberly. "Do you know, I've never had a meal like this cooked for me before?"

"So no woman has tried to make inroads to your heart through your stomach?" she asked in mock horror.

To her surprise, instead of taking a lighter road, he admitted, "Lynnette didn't cook. We had takeout or meals at a local diner, much like Dad does." He paused and added, "And I haven't dated much since then."

And she knew exactly why. Handing him the cobbler, she said, "I'll cook when I can, for your dad, too."

"I think you're going to deserve more than a piece of land when our year is up."

Did that mean he could possibly give her his heart? But then he added, "I might have to raise your salary."

She felt her hopes wither but she wouldn't let him notice. "Try the cobbler," she encouraged brightly.

He did and she did. When she glanced over at him, she saw he was watching her with that deep intensity that darkened his eyes. A ripple of excitement skipped up her spine.

"What?" she asked.

He leaned toward her and stroked his finger above the skin over her lip. "Whipped cream."

She could imagine him using that voice in bed with her. She could imagine him using that voice in between kisses, in between—

He lifted his finger to his lips and licked off the whipped cream he'd taken off hers. Then he leaned closer to her.

Jazzy's insides were all a-twitter. Maybe he was going to kiss her. Maybe she'd actually feel his lips on hers, like she'd dreamt about for so many nights now.

But as soon as she had the thought, he must have realized what he was doing. His expression closed down, that dark, male intensity left his eyes, and he was once again essentially her business partner. Nothing more.

That was it, she thought. She'd have to deal with a year of wanting him to kiss her...a year of wanting more than that.

But she had *her* pride, too. She certainly wouldn't throw herself at him. She wasn't going to set herself up for a huge fall. She'd have to be as calm and practical about this as he was.

Calm and practical, she told herself once again. "We really should get back to your dad's."

Brooks's expression didn't change, though she could feel his body tense beside her. "Just let me get my boots."

As he hiked himself up off the couch and strode toward his bedroom, she whispered to herself once more, "Just be calm and practical, and you'll be fine."

But she didn't believe it.

The next few days sped by as Jazzy manned the phones at Brooks's clinic and tried to forget that he'd almost kissed her, tried to stop asking herself the question—why *hadn't* he kissed her? The day before the wedding, she was getting ready for work in the morning when Cecilia came to her room.

After Jazzy let her friend in, Cecelia said, "I'm kidnapping you this morning."

Jazzy ran her brush through her hair. "What do you mean *kidnapping* me?"

"I told Brooks you had something important to do for the wedding this morning. He said that was fine. There aren't any appointments on Buckskin Clinic's schedule and you could take the morning off."

"Then I really should go check on his dad—"

"Nope. You're going with me to Bea's Beauty Salon. *You* are getting a makeover."

Jazzy spun around. "A *makeover?*"

"A hair trim, some highlighting, and I brought a bunch of makeup along. We're going to get you ready for the wedding."

At first she was going to protest, but then she thought about her relationship with Brooks thus far. She thought he found her attractive, yet something was holding him back. Maybe his past romantic history. Maybe his broken engagement. Maybe he just didn't want to delve under the surface of the murky waters of their business arrangement. Maybe all of the above. But Jazzy knew she wanted more than a marriage on paper. If she was going to be married to Brooks, then she wanted to be *married* to him. She was afraid if she told him that, he'd call off the whole agreement. Possibly this whole deal had made her a little crazy. They certainly hadn't known each other very long. But she felt more sure of this marriage than she'd felt about anything in her life.

"My family's arriving today," she murmured. "Abby and Cade are driving my car up and parking it at Brooks's condo."

"All of your family is coming?"

"Everyone."

"But you don't look as happy about it as you should. What's going on, Jazzy?"

Oh, no. She couldn't confide this marriage of convenience to anyone. Not anyone. Not for her sake, not for Brooks's sake, and not for his dad's sake.

"Just jittery, I guess. Maybe a day at the salon is just what I need," she joked.

She'd never been that fashion-conscious or put much store in spending hours in front of a mirror. But Cecilia didn't wear gobs of makeup and she certainly looked pretty. Maybe she couldn't find a guy because she didn't care about all that as much as she should.

Not that she wanted just any guy anymore. She wanted Brooks Smith.

"I have something I want to show you." Jazzy went to the small closet, reached up for a hanger, and brought out her wedding dress for Cecilia to see. It was a Western-cut, three-quarter length dress with just the right amount of fringe. "I bought it online, what do you think?"

"I think it's *perfect* for you. Oh, Jazzy, you're going to look so pretty."

Jazzy reached up to the shelf above where her clothes were hanging and pulled down a Western hat with a bit of tulle around the brim and down the back. "And this goes with it."

"I'm so glad you showed that to me. We'll keep that in mind when we're getting your hair done. I have you set up for a manicure and a pedicure at the same time. A facial first."

"Cecilia, that's too much."

"Nonsense. It's part of my wedding gift to you…and Brooks," she said with a wink. "Believe me, he'll appreciate it when you're done over."

Done over.

"So what are you wearing tonight for the rehearsal dinner?" Cecilia asked.

"There isn't a rehearsal, per se. We're going to dinner

with our families and then the minister is going over the basics at the church. I'm not having bridesmaids. Jordyn will be my witness. Brooks's dad is going to be his."

"So where are you all going to dinner tonight?"

"The diner. They've reserved a big table. I just hope my family behaves. You know how they can get. Mom tried to talk me out of getting married. Dad asked a lot of questions. Laila, Abby and Annabel would have taken over the ceremony and everything about the reception if I hadn't put my foot down…hard. Brooks and I had everything planned and we knew exactly what we wanted. I wasn't going to let my family mess with that. We don't want a big shindig for Brooks's dad to have to deal with. I've explained that to everyone more than once so I hope they'll be on their best behavior."

"You don't want a fuss or argument that could cause a heart attack."

"Exactly. I'm worried about Barrett as it is, how he's going to be, how he's going to feel, what he's going to think."

"Think about you and Brooks?"

"And about my family's attitude. Barrett actually believes in love at first sight. He and his wife had it. So he's going to be right in there rooting for us. He could be at odds with my parents."

Cecilia suddenly took Jazzy's hand. "Jazzy, what do you want?"

"I want a happy, committed, long-lasting marriage with lots of babies."

"Have you and Brooks talked about babies?"

"No. But we have time." They had a year…at least. She had to be hopeful.

Cecilia ran her hand down the delicate fabric of the

wedding dress and the silky fringe at the sleeves. "This really is magnificent. That means everything that goes with it should be, too. Do you have shoes?"

"High-heeled boots. I ordered those online, too. But they're a little big. I'll stuff tissue in the toes and in the back." Pulling them out from the bottom of the closet, Jazzy showed Cecilia the calf-high boots.

"I was hoping you'd have open-toed shoes, so everyone could see your pedicure."

"It's mid-October in Montana. I don't want my feet to freeze."

Cecilia shrugged. "The boots will make you look sexy. Brooks will still be taller than you, even with those heels."

Actually, Jazzy liked the effect of Brooks towering over her. She liked the fact that when he hugged her, he surrounded her.

"What color for the toenails and fingernails? What will you be wearing *after* the wedding?"

Jazzy certainly hadn't thought about *that,* either. They'd be going back to Brooks's condo. It wasn't as if they were going anywhere special. "I guess I'll wear something I brought along."

"You are not talking flannel pajamas, are you?"

"No, I brought along a nightgown and robe."

"Yeah, I bet it's the kind you feel comfortable in. That's not what you need. Something else we're fitting in this morning. We'll be stopping at the General Store. Nina has a rack of nightgowns and robes. Maybe if there's time when we're done, I'll drive you into Kalispell to a cute little dress shop I know there. You need something special for tonight, too, Jazzy. Something that shows your family you know exactly what you're doing…something that shows this town that this wedding isn't of the shotgun variety."

"Is that what everyone's saying? That I had to get married because I was pregnant?"

"I've heard it at the beauty salon, around the General Store, around the volunteers at the elementary school."

"I hope you squelched it."

"You know each one of those gossip conversations is like a little bonfire. It takes a lot of water to douse them out. The best thing would be seeing you looking slim and confident and ready to go into this marriage as if it's just any other marriage. And it *is* like any other marriage, right?"

Oh, how Jazzy wished that were true. "It's a marriage that Brooks and I will work at to make last."

That's what she had to believe.

That evening when Jazzy took off her coat at the diner, all eyes in the place seemed to be focused on her. Especially Brooks's.

Cecilia had insisted she buy a red dress. The one she'd chosen was simple and sleek enough—even understated with its high neckline and just-above-the-knee hem. But there was a slit in the side and when she turned around, there was a keyhole in the back.

But Brooks wasn't looking at her back; he was looking at her front, and boy, was he looking at her front. Not only the dress, but her hair and her face, too. She'd used mascara, lipstick and some kind of powder that almost shimmered on her skin. With her newly highlighted blond hair tapered around her face in a fresh style, she'd never felt more confident as a woman.

Brooks was looking at her as a very stunned man.

"There she is," Barrett said with a wide smile. "I knew she wouldn't run out on you."

But Brooks didn't seem to hear his father. He couldn't seem to take his eyes off her. And she couldn't take her eyes off him. He'd worn a dressier Western shirt tonight with bolo tie and black jeans with boots. Tall and handsome and ultimately sexy, she found herself trembling just standing there.

"Don't you look beautiful," her mother said, motioning to the chair next to her. "Not that you don't always look pretty, but tonight something's…different."

"She's dressed to bowl over any guy she meets," Brody said, not looking as if he approved.

But she squelched that statement right away. "Only one guy," she assured them all. Was she acting or had she really said that? She meant it.

Brooks stepped closer to her like a fiancé would, took her hand and squeezed it.

Leaning close to her ear, he murmured, "You look gorgeous."

Was he acting, too?

He led her to the chair her mother had gestured to and pulled it out for her. She sank down onto it before her legs gave way. This was some way to start the evening with her head feeling as if it were filled with cotton and her mouth totally dry.

Brooks took his seat next to her and they faced her family. He covered her hand with his again and she knew to everyone gathered there, they looked like a loving couple.

Yet her father was frowning as he stared at them. "So tell me again why you're rushing into this marriage so fast, without giving us all breathing space, and time to get used to the idea."

Her whole family had come—Abby and Jackson, Laila and Cade, Annabel and Thomas, Jordyn Leigh, Brody and her parents. Jazzy knew Jordyn was on her side. After she'd seen the phone picture of Brooks Jazzy had sent her, she'd insisted he was too good to let go. But the rest of her family... She had to make this good.

However, before she could open her mouth, Brooks, protective as ever, stepped in. "I'm not sure you can explain the bond that forms when two people just click, sir, the way Jazzy and I did from the beginning."

That definitely didn't allay her father's concerns. "So you're just going to move up here, away from us, without discussing it with the family?"

Jazzy exchanged looks with Abby, Annabel and Laila who'd gone through the process of falling in love. Her look said *Help me out here, sisters!* Abby did. "You know how true love works, Dad. You've seen me and Laila and Annabel go through it. When it's right, it's right."

"We won't see you very much," her mother said, a little sadly.

Brooks assuaged her mom's concerns. "We'll visit you often. Jazzy's going to want to make sure you're part of our lives, and I will, too." The look he sent Jazzy said he meant that.

"You folks can stay with me the next time you're in town," Barrett told them. "Brooks still considers me an invalid and won't let me overdo anything. I'd be glad to have the company." He stared at Jazzy's dad. "I hear you're good with horses. I've got a few."

The tension around the table eased. The two men

began talking ranch life. Jordyn gave her a thumbs-up sign. Brody, however, eyed her suspiciously as if he still didn't believe what was going on. Her sisters and their husbands fell into conversation, too.

Brooks interlaced his fingers with hers on the table, leaned close and said only loud enough for her to hear, "It's going to be all right."

But as she felt the heat between them, as his breath fanned her cheek, as his gaze unsettled her the way no other could, she thought about her vows tomorrow and wondered if everything *could* be all right.

Chapter Ten

Brooks knew he must be crazy. Today he was going to marry a woman he was seriously attracted to, yet he didn't intend to sleep with her! If that wasn't crazy, he didn't know what was.

He adjusted his tux, straightened his bolo tie, wishing all to heck that Jazzy hadn't almost knocked his boots off last night when he'd seen her in that red dress. And when he pushed her chair in and saw her skin peeking through that cutout in the back, he'd practically swallowed his tongue.

There was a rap on the door. He was in the anteroom that led to the nursery area in the back of the church. He knew Jazzy was in a room across the vestibule that was used exactly for situations like this—brides and their bridesmaids preparing for a wedding.

Preparing for a wedding.

After the dinner last night, and the suspicious and wary glances of her family, he'd retreated inward. He knew that. He also knew it had bothered Jazzy. But how could he explain to her that she turned him on more than he'd ever wanted to be turned on? How could he explain to her that this marriage of convenience might not be so convenient, not when it came to them living together?

Still he was determined to go through with this. Their course was set. He wasn't going to turn back now.

After a deep breath, he opened the door. Jazzy's sister Jordyn stood there with an unsure smile. She'd been the one person to treat him like the brother-in-law he was going to be.

"Everything's all set," she said. "Once you're in place at the altar, the organist will start the processional."

Stepping into the vestibule, he saw his dad beckoning to him from the doorway that would lead up to the altar. He also saw Jazzy's dad looking more like a soldier than a father, standing by the door to the room where she'd emerge.

Mr. Cates frowned at Brooks.

Brody stood at the entrance to the church, his mother on his arm. He was ready to walk her up the aisle. But when he glanced over his shoulder and saw Brooks, his mouth tightened and Brooks saw the disapproval in his eyes.

If he were a betting man, he'd bet that someone in Jazzy's family would stand up and protest at that point in the wedding when the minister asks, "Is there anyone who sees a reason that these two shouldn't be joined in matrimony?"

"Abby, Annabel and Laila will give you a chance," Jordyn assured him as if she could read his thoughts.

"And because *they* will, their husbands will, too. Mom and Dad and Brody will come around as long as they see you make Jazzy happy. And you will, won't you?"

After the way he'd left Jazzy last night, with him all silent and brooding, he'd wanted to do something nice to reassure her. So he'd bought a bottle of champagne to celebrate when they got back to his place tonight. That's when he'd give her the watch. He wanted her to be happy, and he'd do his best to see that happen. But no one could *make* someone else happy. Everyone had choices, and those choices either led to success or failure.

So he was truthful with Jordyn. "I want Jazzy to be happy."

Jordyn gave him an odd look, as if she suspected everything might not be what it seemed. Then she confirmed it when she said, "I trust Jazzy to make the right decisions for herself. I'll be around if she needs me. Don't you hesitate to call me if she *does* need me."

"I won't," he promised, and he meant it.

Brooks crossed the vestibule and approached his father. When they were standing next to each other, Barrett pounded Brooks on the back. "I'm glad you asked me to be your best man. You could have had Gage Christensen or even Dallas Traub, for that matter."

He and Dallas had been friends for years, but since his divorce and gaining custody of his three kids, Dallas had had even less time for friendship than Brooks had.

"I wanted *you,* Dad."

"This day makes me happier and prouder than you'll ever know. Jazzy will be good for you. She'll ground you like your mother grounded me. You and me—we're going to have to have a talk one of these days, about marriage and everything that goes with it."

"I think I learned the facts of life a long time ago, Dad," Brooks said with a smile, trying to lighten the atmosphere a bit.

His father's face grew a little red. "That's not what I mean. There are things…there are just some things we need to talk about."

The minister emerged from behind the altar and Brooks nudged his father's arm. "We can talk. But right now, I think it's time for me to get married."

His father chuckled and side by side, they walked up the aisle to the front of the church.

Jazzy felt like a princess. It was silly, really. This dress wasn't all tulle and lace. It was more like a dressy, Western dress. But it was white and her boots were white with three-inch spiked heels, and Cecilia had made sure her hat was tilted just right on her head with the tulle flowing down the back of her dress. Mostly she felt like a princess because she could see Brooks waiting for her at the altar, all handsome and starched and pressed, with shiny black boots, and a look in his eyes that was lightning hot.

Last night she'd been worried because he'd turned so quiet, so expressionless, so unlike the Brooks she knew. What would he be like today after they were married?

That thrill of anticipation ran down her spine. He was going to be her husband.

Her dad stood beside her and held out the crook of his arm for her to put her hand through. She knew he wasn't on board with this wedding, but she couldn't keep living her life to please her parents. At thirty, it was well past time she flew the coop. She could see her mom sitting in the front pew, her sisters and their husbands in the pew behind that.

Jordyn Leigh, however, was going to lead the way on the road to this future. She'd worn a pretty, royal blue dress that, in Jazzy's estimation, was just right for this ceremony. She and Brooks hadn't wanted pomp and circumstance and long gowns. They'd wanted simple and quiet and just plain friendly.

The organ music began and with a spray of yellow mums clenched in her hands, Jordyn glanced over her shoulder at Jazzy and then started forward.

Jazzy held on to her bouquet of lilies and white mums even more tightly, afraid she'd drop it. She was that nervous. As the scent of the flowers wafted up to her, she used the look in Brooks's eyes as her guiding light. He couldn't look at her like that and not feel something, could he?

Whether he felt something or not, she was going to marry him and see where the future led them. Exciting couldn't even describe the ripple of emotion inside of her. Everything about today was going to be memorable.

Just as she reinforced the thought, Laila turned toward her and snapped a picture with her camera. Abby and Annabel had cameras, too, and knowing her sisters, everything about today would be recorded.

Tears pricked in her eyes. She blinked fast and smiled.

The church aisle really wasn't that long, but her walk down toward the altar seemed to take forever. But she didn't falter as the look in Brooks's eyes drew her forward.

Once Jazzy was at the front of the church, her father solemnly kissed her and she took her place beside Brooks.

"You look beautiful," he said in an almost awed voice.

"You look pretty spiffy yourself."

At her words, the awkwardness they both seemed to be feeling drifted away. He smiled, one of those Brooks smiles that affected her in a way she didn't understand, that made her feel hot and giddy and altogether a woman.

Beside Brooks, his father beamed at Jazzy and in that moment she felt a few doubts about what she was doing. What would happen to Barrett's feelings about her in a year if she and Brooks separated? But she couldn't think about that now. Today they were joining their lives. Somehow this would work out.

The minister welcomed their family and guests.

Jazzy handed her bouquet to Jordyn as she and Brooks joined hands. His was warm and dry and firm, decisive in its hold on hers. She felt fragile and beautiful and supportive beside him. The words of the ceremony became a blur as the minister talked, as she and Brooks responded.

They each said "I do" calmly as if they knew what they were doing.

Then Brooks's voice was low but strong as he said, "I, Brooks Smith, take you Jazzy Cates to be my lawfully wedded wife...to have and to hold from this day forward...for better or for worse...for richer, for poorer...in sickness and health...to love and to cherish until death do us part."

She repeated those same words, looking straight into his eyes so he'd know she meant them. Now his reaction was more stoic, yet the nerve in his jaw worked. The ceremony was affecting him, too. He just didn't want anyone to see that.

As Brooks slipped the gold band onto her finger, she could hardly breathe. When she slipped the gold band onto his finger, a hush over their guests seemed to emphasize the importance of the moment. They held hands and gave their attention to the minister as he said a few words about love and marriage, bonds, promises and a union that made the world go round.

They bowed their heads as the minister bestowed a blessing, and then he said the words the whole church was waiting to hear.

"I now pronounce you husband and wife." In a low voice, he said to Brooks, "You can kiss her now."

Well, of course, they *had* to kiss. They had to show everyone they meant what they'd said…the promises they'd made.

Brooks's arms went around her and there was only a moment of hesitation before he bent his head to her. His lips found hers unerringly as if this had been a long time in coming. She certainly felt as if it had, but then maybe he was just determined to get it over with. Yet as his lips settled on hers, it certainly didn't seem as if he wanted this kiss over with quickly. This meeting of lips took on more than a perfunctory air. It went on longer than she thought it would. In fact, she didn't know how long it went on because she lost track of time and place and the fact that there were guests watching them.

Apparently, Brooks forgot, too, because his arms held her a little tighter and he didn't raise his head and break their kiss until the minister cleared his throat.

She should feel embarrassed, she really should. But

she was so awed by the desire behind what had just happened that she couldn't even think of anything else. She probably couldn't have found her way out of the church. But Jordyn handed back her bouquet. Brooks took her arm and, in the next moment, they were walking down the aisle to the smiles and applause of their family and friends.

She was married. Brooks was her husband. The full reality of that hadn't set in yet.

They walked down the aisle to the back of the church, through the vestibule to the reception hall. Once inside, Brooks took her elbow and spun her around. "I had to do that, Jazzy. I had to make it look good." There was something in his voice that was a little unsettled as if making the kiss look good had unsettled him. And here she'd thought the kiss had really *meant* something.

"You certainly made it look good. I'm not sure what my parents thought of it, but afterward your dad was grinning from ear to ear."

"They'll all be in here in a minute. We just have to be clear about how we're handling it. No honeymoon now because of taking care of Dad's practice, as well as setting up mine. We'll be moving back to Rust Creek Falls as soon as we find a good place. Not a house, though. Not yet."

"Your father's going to think we're planning to build on your grandmother's property."

"I'm not going to tell him we will. If that's what he thinks, fine."

Her hand on his arm, looking up into his eyes, she said, "Brooks, I don't like deceiving anyone, especially not him."

But Brooks didn't have a chance to respond because

their guests started pouring in and they began receiving them like a newly married couple would.

Brooks's dad pounded him on the back, congratulating him. Jazzy's sisters gathered around and gave her a group hug. She and Brooks got separated more than once as guests migrated to their tables and conversations abounded. They had almost greeted the last of their guests and Brooks had stepped aside to speak to the minister, when Dean took Jazzy's arm.

"I can't believe you went through with this so quickly."

"You're going to be doing the same soon."

"That's different and you know it. I'm still getting the feeling that something's off here. That all of this happened too fast."

"Dean, Brooks and I just got married. Why can't you simply wish us well?"

"Maybe you married Brooks to escape Thunder Canyon and your family, but is that a valid reason? Shelby and I are getting married because we can't live without each other."

"Are you judging what I feel?" Dean was an old enough and good enough friend that she could ask the honest question.

He shook his head. "I'm just hoping you're head over heels in love and this isn't something other than that."

Looking him straight in the eye, she assured him, "I'm head over heels in love." That thought still shook her up, made her feel queasy, instilled in her the knowledge that she could easily be terribly hurt.

But it was absolutely true. She loved Brooks Smith.

Dean's eyes widened a bit as he could see the truth.

He gave Jazzy a big hug. "Then congratulations. I hope the two of you have a lot of happy years together."

She was hoping for one year that would stretch into a lifetime.

Jazzy sat beside Brooks during their wedding dinner, wondering what he was thinking. He smiled, but the smile didn't light up his eyes. He spoke to their guests, but there was a surface quality about it that troubled her. Every once in a while, he'd reach over and squeeze her hand or drop his arm around her shoulders. But the gestures felt forced. She just wanted to give him a hug… nestle in his arms. That's what a wife would do when she was feeling unsure.

Jordyn, who had taken over as facilitator for the day—and Jazzy was so grateful because this sister wanted to help, not interfere—tapped Jazzy on the arm and addressed Brooks, too. "It's time to cut the cake. Are you ready?"

She and Brooks hadn't really talked about this…or prepared a script. This would be a go-with-the-flow moment.

Brooks stood without a word and held Jazzy's chair for her. Once she'd gotten to her feet, he took her arm and escorted her to the table where the multilayered cake stood.

"You can have the top layer to take along," Jordyn told them. "For a midnight snack," she teased with a wink as if she imagined what they'd be doing then.

What would they be doing at midnight? Jazzy wondered. Sleeping? Pacing their separate bedrooms, thinking about whether or not they'd done the right thing? How many doubts was her new husband having?

"I bought you a special cake-slicing knife so you'll remember this moment," Jordyn said with a smile and handed them a cake knife with their names and the date engraved on the handle.

"Oh, Jordyn," Jazzy said with tears filling her eyes. "Thank you."

As she hugged her sister, flashes from cameras went off and she realized her family was recording the moment. She heard Brooks sincerely thank Jordyn, too.

Then it was time. With friends and family looking on, Brooks's hand covered hers over the handle of their first wedding gift. There was a stack of presents on the table beside the cake. Even though this was a sudden wedding, their guests were taking the opportunity to give them something to start them on their way.

Brooks's hand was large, warm and encompassing. When he gazed down at her and gave her a half smile, Jazzy's breath hitched.

Brooks himself took care of the slice of cake, sliding it onto a paper plate. Then he offered it to her. They each broke off a piece, knowing what they were supposed to do.

Brooks lifted the bite of cake and icing to her lips, never taking his eyes from hers.

Flashes from cameras again burst around them.

She opened her mouth, and when she took the bite from his fingers, her tongue touched his thumb and icing slid along her upper lip.

The sound of a spoon tapping a glass rung in her ears. As if the sound had to be translated, a woman called, "Kiss that icing away!" More tinkling on glasses. After all, this was a wedding reception.

Brooks leaned in and kissed her. The icing became

the sweetest confection she'd ever tasted as Brooks's tongue slipped along her lips and she kissed him back.

When he broke away, she blinked, tried to find her equilibrium and realized it was *her* turn now. If he kissed her like that again… She was careful picking up his piece of cake. He was careful as he ate it from her fingers. Everyone clapped. She tried to smile along with Brooks as they both seemed to be relieved that tradition was over.

As Jordyn oversaw the slicing of the cake for guests, some of them chatted with Jazzy and Brooks. Dallas Traub, who Brooks had introduced in their receiving line, approached them. "I just want to tell both of you not to be strangers. We've all been so focused on recovering from the flood, we haven't had time for anything else. After spending so much time with my rug rats, I could use adult conversation."

Earlier, Jazzy had learned that Dallas lived on his family's ranch—the Triple T—but had his own house on the property that had seen some damage from the flood, but not the devastation others had experienced.

"I'd like to see your ranch sometime. And meet your children." After all, it was only polite to make Brooks's friend feel comfortable.

"We'll set up a time soon," Dallas assured them. Then he clapped Brooks on the back and walked away.

"He's been through a rough time," Brooks said almost to himself. "That's when family counts most."

Jazzy imagined he was thinking again about the reason for this wedding—not true love, not a lifelong commitment, but rather his dad's health.

Had they done the right thing?

* * *

A short time later, as Brooks and Jazzy were mingling with their guests, Brooks watched Jordyn go to the podium and pick up the microphone. She tapped it and smiled. "It's time for the first dance between Jazzy and Brooks as a married couple," she announced. Turning to the CD player on the wall, she started the music.

It was one dance, Brooks thought, as he offered his hand to Jazzy. Surely he could get through one dance.

He thought of the first time he and Jazzy had danced when they'd looked over the social hall. And their kiss after the ceremony, not to mention the sensual tasting of the wedding cake—

He had to look at this logically. This day was simply an exception to the agreement they had made. Today, they were pretending in front of a larger audience than his dad. Today would be over before they knew it.

His wedding day. When he'd imagined it with Lynnette, he'd had dreams. Now he just wanted his dad's good health. He just wanted the year to pass quickly so he and Jazzy could get on with their lives.

As Brooks forced a smile and took Jazzy in his arms, he was glad they'd had that one practice dance. That way this wasn't so awkward.

Just like last night when Jazzy had appeared in the diner in her red dress, he'd been bowled over by the way she'd looked in her wedding dress as she'd walked down the aisle on her father's arm. It was so feminine with its lace and high neck. Yet it had a touch of Western sass, too, with its fringes and peek-a-boo sections that gave him a glimpse of skin. And those boots with their heels...

Taking her in his arms and bending his head to her,

he said, "I don't know how you can dance in those things."

"These boots were made for dancing," she joked, but her smile wobbled just enough that he knew this day wasn't easy for her, either. He was glad he'd bought the roses, champagne and watch for tonight.

When he leaned toward her, he got caught in the fragrance of her perfume. It was musky-sweet and fit Jazzy perfectly. "Are you okay?" he asked seriously, in spite of everyone watching.

"As okay as you," she returned with her usual spunk. But then she added, "Though I'm glad we're not in a fishbowl all the time. It's downright unnerving."

"Now you know how celebrities feel," he bantered, hoping to make her smile again.

She didn't just smile. She laughed. And he realized how much he enjoyed the sound of it.

"Maybe I should simply think of my family as groupies!"

Flashes popped as both Laila and Abby took photos of them.

"They're going to make an album for us." Jazzy was watching him for his reaction.

"Your family is just doing what families do."

"Maybe we should have gotten married by the justice of the peace. It would have been simpler the whole way around," she murmured.

Tearing his gaze from Jazzy's, he caught sight of his father watching them. His broad smile said it all.

"Just look at my dad, Jazzy." He maneuvered them so she could see Barrett.

After the moment it took for her to absorb his message, she sighed.

Brooks didn't know what that sigh meant because everyone began clinking their spoons on their glasses so he and Jazzy would kiss.

"Here we go again," he said, tightening his arms around her, drawing her close so her body was pressed against his. She didn't resist or try to lean away.

When his lips met hers, he intended to make the kiss quick. He intended for it to simply be a brushing of lips on lips.

But with Jazzy, nothing was ever exactly as he intended it to be.

Her perfume was like a magic spell, drawing him into its aura. Jazzy was so femininely alluring, his hand came up to caress her cheek. Careful not to disturb her hat, he angled his mouth over hers and almost forgot about "pretend." His lips felt so right on hers.

In the nick of time, before he took their public kiss into the private realm, he pulled away. Jazzy almost tripped over his boot and he caught her up against him so they didn't have a mishap.

Charlie called out, "Careful those kisses don't knock you off your feet!"

Everyone laughed. Everyone except him and Jazzy. They couldn't seem to unlock their gazes.

And they didn't until Jordyn announced, "Now my dad will dance with Jazzy and Brooks will dance with my mom. Everyone else, join in and enjoy the music."

Brooks had to let Jazzy go. Tearing his gaze from hers, he realized he didn't like that idea at all.

That night on the porch at Brooks's condo, Jazzy held the top layer of foil-wrapped wedding cake, still not quite believing what had taken place. She and Brooks had said their vows, he'd kissed her so passionately her hat had almost popped off. When he'd licked that icing—

He set her suitcase down on the porch and unlocked the door, glancing at her. "You packed light when you came to Rust Creek Falls. One suitcase? Most women would have three."

"I'm not most women." She wanted to say, "I'm your wife now," but she didn't.

He gave her a very long look that made her shift the layer of cake from one hand to the other, then he opened the door.

Jazzy caught the scent of roses as soon as she walked inside. Immediately she spotted the vase on the side table and went straight to it. The blooms were huge and red, giving off a beautiful scent.

"They're wonderful!"

"I thought you might like them."

She wanted to cross to him and kiss him all over again in a way that wasn't simply for show, but she didn't have that freedom.

While he carried her suitcase to the guest bedroom, she looked around the place and noticed a fire was laid on the grate. Maybe they'd cozy up together in front of it.

Brooks returned to the living room. "I'll light a fire. I have champagne, too. We can celebrate. I've never seen my dad happier."

His dad. That was the reason they'd done this, and she couldn't forget it. "Champagne would be nice," she agreed.

When Brooks started for the kitchen, she followed with the cake. "I'll find a plate."

"Top left cupboard. You'll have to learn your way around," he said with a smile.

That smile. She sighed, found two plates and unwrapped the cake.

Five minutes later they were sitting on the sofa with a fire dancing on the grate, sharing bites of cake. Brooks had taken off his jacket and rolled up his sleeves.

"It was a nice wedding," she said as a preamble.

"Yes, it was," he agreed. "But I'm not sure your parents approve of me, or your brother, either."

Her dad had questioned Brooks about his practice and so had her brother. They hadn't smiled much and Jazzy wished, as she had in the past, that they'd just trust her judgment.

Brooks took the bottle of champagne he'd pulled from the refrigerator, unwrapped the foil around the top, and then popped the cork. It bounced across the room and they both laughed. He poured the champagne into two tumblers, only filling them about a third of the way. As he picked up her glass, as well as his, and handed it to her, the bubbles danced and popped.

"Before today, I hadn't had champagne since my sister's wedding."

"Then it's about time." He clinked his glass against hers. "We pulled it off."

Yes, they had. "My parents will be harder to convince if and when we visit them."

"It will be fine, Jazzy, really it will. Jordyn's on our side. She still lives at home, right?"

Jazzy nodded and took a couple of swallows of her champagne. "She'll be a good buffer. I wish I could confide in her, but it's difficult for sisters to keep secrets from one another. I'm afraid if I tell her, she'll tell Abby, Abby will tell Laila, Laila will tell Annabel..."

"You can talk to *me*."

Yes, she could talk to Brooks about everything but what she felt for him. She took another swallow of champagne and realized she'd drained her glass. He drank his, too, picked up the bottle, and poured more for both of them. They were sitting close together, the sleeve of her dress rubbing the sleeve of his shirt, their knees brushing every now and then.

"I spoke to Charlie tonight," she said.

"He keeps Dad on track as much as he can."

"Did he tell you your dad wants to do the chores himself?" Jazzy asked him. "He doesn't want Travis helping him."

"Travis has his orders from *me*. He's supposed to listen to me, not to Dad."

"Charlie insists your dad's stubborn."

"He doesn't know how to sit still unless his favorite program's on the TV," Brooks grumbled. "He's eating the meals you're making him, though. That's a good sign. And he walks up and down the drive, going farther each day. When bad weather sets in, I don't know what he'll do. Maybe I can get him a treadmill for Christmas."

"Do you think he'd use it?"

"I can set it up in the basement and make him a gym area. If I have to, I'll go there and work out with him."

She drank more champagne, then laid her hand on Brooks's arm. His forearm was as muscled as the rest of him, the dark brown hair there was rough under her fingertips. "You're a good son."

"We haven't been close enough in my adult years. Maybe now that will change."

"I think it will…if you both want it to."

Brooks reached to the shelf under the coffee table and brought out a wrapped package. She hadn't noticed it under there, though now the gold foil gleamed in the lamplight.

"Brooks, what's this?"

"Just a little something for you to remember today. Open it."

Jazzy's fingers fumbled as she tore the paper off the box with a Western scene. "Montana Silversmiths." Taking the lid from the box, she saw the watch inside. Lifting it out, she examined the scrollwork on the band, the pretty face.

"Oh, Brooks, it's beautiful! Thank you."

"Put it on and see if it fits."

It fit her wrist as if it had been made for her.

Brooks poured more champagne into the two glasses. Then he looked at her as he'd looked at her when she'd walked up the aisle toward him, when she'd taken his hand and faced the minister. "You've been a good sport about all of this."

"I have a dream, too," she said, knowing Brooks would think she was talking about the rescue ranch, not about their marriage.

The longer they gazed at each other, the more the fire crackled and popped, the more the electric tension in the air seemed to draw them together. She didn't want this moment of closeness to end. Maybe those champagne bubbles had gone to her head, but she thought she saw desire in his eyes.

He took a strand of her hair in his hand and then

played with it between his fingers. "So silky and soft. In that hat and your dress, you looked as if you'd just stepped off the pages of a fashion magazine."

"I'm just Jazzy," she said with a small laugh, feeling all trembly inside. "The same girl who got to know Sparky because of you. The same girl who got scratched by Mrs. Oliver's cat. The same girl who will never be a calf roper."

He laughed at that and leaned a little closer. "I have no doubt you could be a calf roper if you set your mind to it."

"I'd rather set my mind on other things."

It seemed as if he would, too, because instead of just touching her hair, his hand delved under it and slid up the back of her neck. She tilted her head up to gaze into his eyes and he leaned even closer.

Something in the air changed. Instead of conversation and banter, Brooks seemed to want something else, and so did she. The kiss after their ceremony flashed in her mind, right before his lips settled on hers. Their kiss with the taste of icing between them was still a sweet memory. But this time as he kissed her, he didn't stop with the pressing of lips on lips or a slight lick of his tongue. Now Brooks's tongue slid along her lips, and she didn't hesitate a second. She opened her mouth to him. He tasted her and she tasted him. He was champagne and icing, and she was tempted by both.

Apparently, he was, too, because his tongue explored her mouth, searching, asking, maybe even demanding. She gave in to his desire…and hers. She responded with everything she had. Her arm went around him and she became intoxicated by the scent of his cologne and the scent of him and the idea that they were husband and wife. She could feel every bit of Brooks's desire. When his fingers went to the zipper on the back of her dress, she anticipated what might happen next. But the sound of the rasp of the metal changed everything. Brooks's fingers froze as he did, too.

He broke their kiss, raised his head and looked as if he'd done something terribly wrong.

Before she could tell him that she liked what they were doing, that after all, they were married, that maybe something new could come of their partnership, he gruffly said, "I'm sorry, Jazzy. I know we have an arrangement and I never intended for this to happen. I just wanted to celebrate a little and show you how much I appreciate what you're doing. This is essentially a business deal, and neither of us should forget that."

A business deal. She'd really never thought of this as strictly business, but clearly, *he* had. The flowers and the champagne and watch were just to show his appreciation.

And the kiss? Well...

She was a woman and he was a man, and he had needs that he apparently wasn't going to satisfy.

"I guess the champagne went to our heads," she murmured.

"I guess," he said gruffly.

"Thank you for the watch. I really like it."

"Good."

So Brooks had once again turned into the monosyllabic remote man he'd been the night before their wedding. Because he felt he'd done something wrong?

So she said the one thing that she knew would make this easier for both of them. "I'd better turn in. I have to unpack and…set up my alarm. Do you want me to go to your dad's with you in the morning?"

"That's up to you."

"I'll go with you. We wouldn't want him to think something's wrong." She stood, feeling a little shaky from everything that had happened today, just wanting to make a fast exit.

He stood, too. "I'll have to make sure the fire's out, so I might be up for a little bit. Good night, Jazzy."

She murmured, "Good night," and headed for her room. As she did, she felt the air on the back of her neck where her zipper had been lowered a bit, and she wondered just what would have happened if both of them had had one more glass of champagne.

Chapter Eleven

The next morning, breakfast was awkward and quick. Jazzy cooked scrambled eggs while Brooks fried bacon. She put the toast in and waited for it to pop while he took everything to the table.

Halfway through eating, Brooks said, "You don't have to go along to check on Dad. I can drop you at the clinic."

That certainly would be easier with this tension between them but not necessarily the best thing to do. "I don't mind. Besides, wouldn't your dad think it was odd that we weren't together the day after our wedding?"

As she'd watched yesterday, Brooks had done some fast talking to both their parents about why they weren't taking a honeymoon yet—what with setting up both clinics and so much to do, they thought they'd wait. With a sigh, Jazzy realized she didn't even know where

Brooks would like to *go* on a honeymoon. She wouldn't care. Anyplace holed up alone with him overnight would be terrific.

If last night had really been their honeymoon—

Once outside in Brooks's truck, their gazes met and she could easily see Brooks was thinking about last night's kiss, too. Yet he obviously didn't want to talk about it or their marriage. He started the truck and aimed it in the right direction.

This tension between them was more than she'd bargained for. This tension between them felt as if it could explode at any moment. She just hoped when it did, they were both ready for the consequences.

When they arrived at the Bar S, Brooks pulled around back to the clinic. But when he rounded the curve in the driveway, he spotted his dad's truck and his father climbing into it.

"What the hell?" he mumbled, as if this was one more stress he didn't need.

Jazzy clasped his arm. "He might be just driving into town to get something at the General Store. His doctor said it was safe for him to drive."

"Jazzy, I know what the doctor said," Brooks snapped. "But I also know Dad always pushes the boundaries, so it's never as simple as it seems. He wouldn't have driven the truck around back unless he wanted to load up a few supplies. I know him. You don't."

That stung because she felt as if she'd come to know Barrett pretty well over the past couple of weeks. True, she didn't know all of his habits, but she did know he wanted to feel better. The two of them had talked about what he needed to do for that to happen. She was hurt Brooks would dismiss her so cavalierly.

"I might not know your dad as well as you do, but during the time we spent together, we talked, probably more than you've talked to him in the past few years."

Brooks looked startled at that observation, but he obviously didn't want to have a conversation about it now. He climbed out of the truck and jogged over to his dad.

Jazzy got out and followed him. All right, so she was going to let *him* handle it. Let's see how well he did that.

"Where are you going this early, Dad?"

With the door to his truck hanging open, Barrett looked from Brooks to Jazzy. "The better question is, what are you two doing here so early? It seems to me you'd be late on the day after your wedding." There was a twinkle of slyness in his eyes that made Jazzy feel uncomfortable.

"Off-topic, Dad. Where are you headed to?"

"It's not like I'm going to drive across the state. Stewart Young called. He has a horse that went lame and he wants me to look at him."

"I can do that," Brooks said in an even voice that told Jazzy he was keeping what he really thought under control.

"Stewart doesn't want *you,* he wants *me. I'm* the one who's handled his horses for thirty years. *I'm* the one he trusts. Besides, I've got to start getting out again. I'm not going to sit in that house like an invalid. That's no better for me than doing too much."

In a way, Jazzy knew he was right. Yet she could also see Brooks was afraid his dad would do something he shouldn't, get involved in something he shouldn't, overexert himself in a way he shouldn't.

Mediating, she suggested, "Why don't both of you go?"

They both swung their gazes toward her in a challenging way. All right, she'd take on two Smith men at once if she had to.

Focusing on Brooks's dad, she suggested, "You can consult with Stewart while Brooks does the actual physical exam. That way you can get out, but Brooks won't worry about you. I can hold down the fort here until you get back. If something comes up at Brooks's clinic, I'll call you. That's what cell phones are made for."

Barrett didn't look happy but he wasn't protesting, either. Still, he eyed them suspiciously. "So tell me again why you're here so early."

Brooks pushed up the rim of his Stetson. "We're here early so maybe we can finish early."

Barrett harrumphed. "I guess the whole evening together would suit the two of you." He noticed the watch on Jazzy's wrist. "That's pretty."

"It was a wedding gift from Brooks." She knew that would please Barrett.

"It's good to know my son *does* have a romantic bone in his body. I guess there's hope."

When Jazzy looked down at the watch, but then back at Brooks's expression, she wasn't so sure.

With troubling insight, Brooks realized whenever he was with Jazzy, he felt like a different person. Sometimes stronger. Sometimes way too unsettled. Their kiss last night weighed on his mind. His brusque attitude this morning did, too. Somehow they had to figure out this marriage.

After his visit to Stewart Young, he'd dropped her

at the Buckskin Clinic. She'd taken care of calls that had come in and referred patients to his dad's clinic where Brooks could see them. It was all a bit confusing for now, but they'd get into a routine, and slowly as his dad came back to work, he'd spend more time at his own clinic.

Eventually his father would say to him, "Let's join our practices," and then they'd get a partner that would take some of the load off them both. It was easy to see the way this should go. He just wished his dad wasn't being so stubborn about it.

After he finished at his dad's, he picked up Jazzy. On the drive home, they decided to order pizza instead of worrying about cooking. They'd been silent in the truck again, though, and Brooks wished they could get back the easy camaraderie they'd had at the beginning of their relationship. What had happened to their friendship?

It had gotten sidetracked by circumstances that had taken on a life of their own.

At his place, he decided against a fire tonight. No more cozy atmosphere. No more thinking about pleasing Jazzy with flowers or champagne. That had given off the wrong signals. He wasn't interested in romance, he told himself, just in an easy companionship between them. Jazzy got herself a glass of water, and he called the pizza establishment he favored most.

He put his hand over the phone. "What do you want on your pizza?"

"It doesn't matter," she said without her usual enthusiasm.

"Tell me *something,* Jazzy, or I'm going to load it up with what I want."

"Pepperoni," she shot at him. "And plenty of onions."

Okay, so she wasn't interested in romance, either.

After he placed the order, she said, "I'm going to give Jordyn a call in my room. Let me know when the pizza arrives."

Before he could blink, she was gone from the kitchen into her bedroom and had closed the door.

For some reason, that closed door annoyed him. Not that he wanted to listen in on her conversation, but it set up another barrier between them.

Restless, he grabbed two plates and set them on the table. Then he rummaged in the drawer for silverware and pulled napkins from the counter. Next on his list was to find an apartment in Rust Creek Falls. It would definitely be more convenient. He could call Rhonda Deatrick now and leave a message. Going to the phone again, he was about to do that, when his doorbell rang.

Couldn't be the pizza already.

When he opened the door to Gage Christensen, he smiled. He'd invited Gage to the wedding but he hadn't been ther

"I kno   didn't show up for the big shindig. I had an emergency call and had to go out. And Lissa's in New York. So I thought I'd stop by now and congratulate you both." He had a package in his hands. "Something I thought you could use other than a toaster."

"Come on in." But as soon as Brooks said it, he realized he shouldn't have. Not because he didn't want Gage there, but because Jazzy was in her own room, not his master suite. Gage had been here before. He knew the setup.

At that moment, Jazzy emerged from the guest bedroom. When she saw Gage, she stopped. Gage handed her the wedding present, but exchanged a look with Brooks.

"You two haven't known each other very long. You weren't dating when Jazzy and I had dinner."

They both kept silent.

"You fell hard overnight?"

"Didn't *you?*" Brooks shot back.

Gage's face turned ruddy. "Maybe. I suppose it does happen." After another long look at both of them, he said, "If the two of you need to talk about anything, I'm around."

Suddenly, his cell phone beeped. He gave a shrug and said, "Excuse me," and checked it. "I've got to get back to the office. Now."

Halfway to the door, he stopped. "Are you coming to the meeting tomorrow night at the town hall? Nate Crawford is supposed to have an important announcement."

They hadn't talked about it, but the meeting would give them something to think about other than this marriage of convenience. "Sure, we'll be there," Brooks responded.

After Gage was gone, Jazzy looked at Brooks. "Do you think he guessed that…this isn't a real marriage? Are we doing the best thing for everyone?" she asked.

"It's too late to have second thoughts now." Though he *was* having second thoughts. Being married to Jazzy for a year and keeping his hands off her was going to be torture.

"Why don't you open Gage's present? We really should open the rest of the stack tonight."

Jazzy sat on the sofa, the box in front of her on the

coffee table. She tore off the wrappings and on the outside of the box they could read PRESSURE COOKER.

"Oh, it's one of those advanced foodie pressure cookers that're supposed to be easy. You can brown everything right in it then let it steam. A meal is supposed to be ready in about half the time," she explained.

"Sounds practical."

"Gage put some thought into this. It's a great newlywed gift."

Yes, it was. When Gage had decided on it for them, he hadn't realized how appropriate it would be. A pressure cooker. Brooks felt as if he were inside a pressure cooker right now, just waiting for it to blow.

The community meeting was just getting underway when Brooks and Jazzy slipped inside the town hall. Jazzy kept stealing glances at Brooks to try to guess what he was thinking. Gage's visit stretched like a wire between them. Was what they were doing wrong, or simply advantageous to them both, as well as Brooks's dad? She wasn't sure anymore. But if it was right, why didn't it feel right?

The folding chairs were packed tight together to fit the most people in. Jazzy's shoulder rubbed against Brooks's but he didn't look her way, though she did look his. He'd dropped her at his clinic this morning while he went to his dad's. All of the appointments Jazzy had made for Brooks at Buckskin Clinic were set up for tomorrow. That seemed to be the easiest way to handle this for now. So they'd be working together tomorrow. Maybe some of this tension would dissipate then.

Irene Murphy saw them and waved. "Congratulations," she called, a few feet from where she was sitting.

A gentleman seated in back of them clapped Brooks on the shoulder and wished them all the best, too. Gage was across the room and just raised his brows. Jazzy didn't know what he was thinking.

Nate Crawford was running the meeting. He banged his gavel on the podium for some order. After thanking everyone for coming, he read a list of the community's accomplishments since the flood. Utilities had been restored, roads repaired, bridges rebuilt.

He went on, talking about the progress on the elementary school and how volunteers had come from all over to help.

The side door to the town hall opened and shut. To distract her attention from Brooks, Jazzy turned to look to see who the newcomers were. A couple walked in followed by—

Jazzy felt her whole body go a little cold. Oh, my. What was Griff Wellington doing here?

As if his eyes were drawn by a magnet, they came to rest on her. It didn't take a genius to figure out he was here to see her. He must have heard about her marriage.

Nate was still speaking and everyone was listening to him. Jazzy raised her hand to Griff, an acknowledgement that she'd seen him, but she wasn't going to disrupt the meeting to go to him. That would look odd.

Brooks nudged her shoulder. "Who's that?"

Maybe he was as aware of her as she was of him. She stayed silent, trying to figure out how to explain.

Before she could, Brooks noted, "You've gone pale."

"Don't be silly. It's just a little cold in here."

"Not with all these people, it isn't. Who is that guy?"

Some of the other meeting-goers had turned to look

at them. Jazzy whispered, "Not now. I'll explain later, okay?"

Brooks gave her a look that said he would indeed expect an explanation later. She wished now she had told him about Griff and her almost-engagement. She wished now she'd told Brooks *she'd* broken it off. But it just hadn't seemed important. Or had the real reason for not telling him been she didn't want him comparing her to the fiancée who had broken her engagement with *him*. Whatever the reason, the die was cast and she'd have to figure this out as she went.

She felt Brooks's gaze on her from the side and she felt Griff's gaze on her from the back. He must have found a seat behind them. The hairs on her neck prickled and she had the feeling she was in for a stormy night. Not at all what she'd planned. She'd hoped she and Brooks could talk and maybe get back on an easy footing. But now this.

Jazzy tried to concentrate on Nate's words once more.

"The reason we called this meeting tonight, the main one, anyway, is that I have some good news for this town. Lissa Roarke's blog and personal diary about life in Rust Creek Falls since the flood has gotten some attention back in New York City. She's going to be on a national morning talk show. I spoke with her myself this afternoon, and she believes that once she's on that show, donations and even more help are going to come rolling in, which will be an even greater help with the reconstruction efforts. So maybe we can really be the town we were before the flood, even better."

Everyone applauded. Gage looked proud enough of

Lissa to burst. But all Jazzy could think of was Griff standing in the back of the hall, waiting for her.

Jazzy grew more antsy the longer the meeting went on. Brooks glanced at her more than once, and she tried to stay calm. She realized, although she'd dated Griff, she didn't really know him very well because she didn't know why he was here and she had no idea what his reaction was going to be to seeing her, to talking with her, to hearing the news of her marriage, if he hadn't heard it yet. But she did know Brooks and the fact that she hadn't told him about Griff weighed heavily on her.

After the road construction foreman spoke, after a couple of ranchers had their say about what they still needed to get their places back to running in top shape, after Nate thanked everyone for coming, the meeting finally ended.

Jazzy tapped Brooks's arm. "I have to speak to someone. It will only be a few minutes."

After Brooks gave her a piercing look, she added, "I'll be right back." Then she slipped away before he could ask her any questions.

When Griff saw Jazzy, his expression was somber. "Can we step outside?"

This was a small town full of people who knew each other. At gatherings like this, they liked to chat. They started forming groups now, doing just that.

Jazzy nodded. Though she started to follow Griff, she glanced back over her shoulder and saw that Brooks's gaze was tracking her.

Once outside, Jazzy glanced up at the beautiful full moon that was lighting up the front of the town hall. It was a momentary distraction before she had to face Griff. However, squaring her shoulders, she did.

"How are you?" she asked.

"I'm good. How are *you?*"

"I'm great," she said brightly, but then dropped the pretense. "Why are you here, Griff?"

"I ran into Abby, or rather she ran into me at the store. She made some excuse about needing new running shoes, but I don't think she runs, does she?"

"She might have taken it up lately." Jazzy always defended her sisters and brother, no matter what.

He nodded his head in concession. "Fair enough. Anyway, she told me you got married. I couldn't believe it. I wanted to ask you myself. Is it true?"

"She wouldn't have lied to you."

Griff looked up into the thousand stars, and then back at her. "No, I suppose not. Is it that guy you were sitting next to?"

"Yes, Brooks Smith. He has a veterinary practice."

"Ah," Griff responded, as if that made sense somehow. "A love of animals. Is that what bonded you together? This is awful quick."

"A love of animals is one of the things that brought us together."

"You never looked at me the way you look at him."

"Griff, don't."

He sighed. "I should have seen our breakup coming. But I guess I was just hoping that I was as right for you as you seemed to be for me."

"Was I really *right* for you? Think about it. We became friends, but—"

"We never had grand passion? I suppose not. Maybe I just wanted to settle down and start a family so badly that I ignored what I *should* have in favor of what we *did* have."

Jazzy had shared embraces and kisses with Griff, details of their lives, the hopes for a future, so it didn't seem odd for her to take his hand now. "I never wanted to hurt you. That's why I broke off our involvement when I did. Don't you see?"

"And you didn't know this Brooks Smith before you left Thunder Canyon?"

"Oh, no! I never would have dated another man behind your back."

"I didn't think so, but I had to have that question answered, too. So you love him?"

"More each day."

Griff gazed into her eyes for a moment, squeezed her hand, then leaned in and kissed her on the cheek. "I wish you well, Jasmine Cates Smith, I really do. Once I get over some hurt pride, maybe when you come back to Thunder Canyon, we can stay friends, and I can meet your guy."

Leaning away, she responded, "I'd like that."

Griff gave her a little salute and then he walked away. She watched after him, knowing he was a good man, knowing he'd make someone a wonderful husband.

She jumped when Brooks's voice startled her. "So... who is he?"

Jazzy glanced around at the people who had started to trickle out of the town hall. Nina Crawford stopped and said to the two of them, "Congratulations on your wedding." She whispered to Brooks, "Even if you don't think you're going to vote for Nate." She'd moved away when another burly gentleman waved to Brooks.

"Can we talk about this when we get home?" Jazzy asked. "A little privacy would be good."

"We can talk in the truck. I don't think I want to wait until we get home."

He was right about that. Or maybe he just didn't want to have to look at her while they were having the talk. He'd have to keep his eyes on the road.

They had parked some ways down the street and they walked that way on what Jazzy knew could be a romantic evening, with that big, full moon and all the stars.

Brooks waited until they were in his truck, buckled up, and then out on the road toward Kalispell. "So spill it," he said in a brook-no-argument voice.

She figured the best way to tell it was just to tell it. "Griff and I dated back in Thunder Canyon."

"Dated, or were dating when you left?"

"Past tense. Laila saw him looking at engagement rings and she told me. He and I had been going out for a few months and I just didn't feel— I just knew he wasn't the one. So I broke off our relationship." She could see Brooks's mouth tighten, his hands wrap more securely around the steering wheel.

"So he thought you were serious enough to get married, and then you broke up with him."

She knew what he was comparing this to. "It's nothing like your relationship with Lynnette."

"Isn't it? And even if it isn't, you didn't tell me about it. I thought you were an honest woman, Jazzy."

That hurt. It hurt terribly. "I *am* honest. I *was* honest. Did you want me to tell you about everyone I dated in the last five years?"

"I told you about Lynnette."

Yes, he had confided in her about his fiancée, and why hadn't she told him about Griff?

"Brooks, I didn't intentionally keep it from you. It

just never came up. It didn't seem important." Not after she'd met him. Not after she'd realized the difference in being around Brooks. It had been nothing like being around Griff.

But she could see he wasn't buying it. She could see he still thought she'd been dishonest with him. There was really no way to change his mind.

When they arrived back at Brooks's place—Jazzy couldn't quite think of it as home yet—he took off his jacket and went to the kitchen. There he pulled a bottle of beer from the refrigerator.

Jazzy followed. "We can talk about this more if you want."

"There's nothing to say, Jazzy. You lied by omission. I don't know if I can forget that."

"Maybe I did it because I didn't want you comparing our friendship or relationship or whatever it is, to yours and Lynnette's."

He gave her a hard stare and unscrewed the cap of the bottle. "That's an excuse but I don't know if it's a good one."

If he understood she'd been falling in love with him, it might be, but she certainly couldn't tell him that now.

"I didn't tell you about Griff because it was over, because I had started a new life here in Rust Creek Falls. You're acting so self-righteous, telling me I'm not an honest woman. Yet you're lying to your father. *We're* lying to your father. How do you account for that? Are *you* a dishonest man?"

He looked totally taken aback as if he'd never put those things in the same category. "That's not the same at all, Jazzy, and you know it. My dad's health was at stake."

"And your relationship with him, and my relationship with my family and friends, too. Maybe my relationship with you is at stake here. Think about it, Brooks, then tell me if we're so different."

His attitude rankled. He was as stubborn as his father. But she loved him, anyway. That, most of all, was what made her turn away. That, most of all, was what made her hightail it out of the kitchen and head for the guest room.

Chapter Twelve

Jazzy stood in the exam room beside Brooks, their bodies not touching if they could help it. She was there because she was more aid to Maggie Bradshaw and her son Timmy who'd brought a rescued kitten in than she was to the vet who had only monosyllabic replies to anything she said. Well, two could play that game. There wouldn't be any conversation. There wouldn't be any closeness. There might not even be a marriage of convenience for much longer.

The little boy, who was about five, was crying. "Momma says if she's sick, we can't keep her!"

Brooks knelt down beside Timmy, making eye contact. "When you first brought her in, I took a blood sample to do testing. I'll find out in a few minutes whether she's sick or not. So how about if you wipe those tears until we find out if we have something to worry about?

I'm giving her a flea treatment, but I have a little comb here, and I'd like to show you how to use it. Do you think you could do that?"

Timmy looked at Brooks as if he'd given him the biggest job in the world. "I can do that."

Brooks nodded to Jazzy. "Can you help him with that?"

It was the first, since last night, that his voice had held a little bit of tenderness…that gentleness she knew so well.

"Sure, I can. I have a stepstool over here, Timmy. You can climb up on that and you'll be right in line with the table."

Timmy glanced over his shoulder at his mom. "I want to keep her."

His mom looked pained as if she wanted to say yes, but yet didn't know if she could take care of a sick cat. The fuzzy, yellow tabby hadn't shown any symptoms yet, but she was only about a month old, and had somehow survived the outdoors. Maybe she was sturdier than she appeared.

"We think she's been sleeping under our porch," Mrs. Bradshaw said. "Timmy came in and got me as soon as he saw her so we could feed her, and she was hungry. If we keep her, is there anything we should know about food?"

"Food in small portions with water in between. Always make sure she has plenty of water, and make sure it's kitten food," Jazzy instructed, then she checked with Brooks. "Right?"

"Right on," he admitted. "I'll go check on the test."

Jazzy showed Timmy how to lift the comb through the fine fur, looking deep at its roots for dirt and any fleas they might find. In about twelve hours, the treatment would take care of the pests, but it would be good to get the dirt out.

Jazzy explained, "In three days, you should give her a bath in no-tears baby shampoo with tepid water, a warm room, and a nice fluffy towel for drying afterward. Some cats don't mind a bath as much as you think. You might want to have a pitcher of water there to pour over her to rinse her. It would be better to start in the morning so she could dry off in a patch of sunlight."

A short while later Brooks was back and he was smiling. "She tested negative for feline leukemia and FIV."

"I told her about the bath," Jazzy said.

He glanced at her. "Right. I understand you don't have any other animals?" he asked Mrs. Bradshaw.

"No, we don't. With food costs the way they are, it just seemed better not to. But this little one found us."

"Do you have a room you can keep her in for the next couple of days? One that you'll be able to clean up fairly well, just in case a flea or two escape."

"We have a sunroom. Would that be all right?"

"In October, that should be perfect. Keeping her there will serve two purposes. It will make sure the fleas are gone. You can also give her a small space to explore a little at a time. In a few days, she'll learn every aspect of that room, then she'll be ready to go exploring elsewhere. She's scared, dehydrated and malnourished, so she's going to need a few days to perk up and feel like her real kitten self again. You're sure there weren't any other kittens close by?"

"Not that we could find. And we did look."

Brooks plucked the kitten from the table and knelt down again in front of the boy. The kitten had curled in Brooks's arm looking up at him with little golden eyes that were trusting and innocent. "Want to hold her?" Brooks asked.

It was obvious Timmy did, but hadn't known if he should. Now, however, Brooks helped him and showed him the best way to hold the kitten so she wouldn't slip away.

"This is good when she's sleepy," he said. "If she gets squirmy, just forget holding her and let her down. She won't want anyone to hold her then and she'll be able to get away, no matter what you do. But when she's sleepy, she'll probably want to cuddle with you."

Timmy looked at his mom. "Can she sleep on my bed, Mommy? Please...please?"

"Maybe it will be a good idea if she does," Mrs. Bradshaw answered. "You won't be so lonely. Ever since his dad left, he's had bad dreams."

"I'm sorry to hear about your husband leaving Rust Creek Falls," Brooks empathized. "You're certain he's not coming back?"

"This place was just too small for him to begin with. He never stayed in one place long before I met him. We came from New Mexico."

"That's a long way," Jazzy said.

"Oh, we stayed in a few states in between, but when we got here, I settled in. I joined a quilting club and a knitting club. Jay wasn't enamored with the place *before* the flood. After the flood, he said there was simply no reason to stay. But I disagreed. Now more than ever, this is a real community. We have to stick together. But he didn't see that. He just wanted to go his own way and said it was time."

"I'm sorry," Jazzy said.

"Being a single mom isn't so bad," she said to Jazzy. "I don't have to consult anyone else about my decisions. But Timmy misses him, and maybe this kitty is the answer to a prayer."

"What are you going to name her?" Jazzy asked.

"Porch," Timmy answered quickly, as if he'd already thought about it. "That's where we found her. Wouldn't that be a good name?"

Brooks laughed. "I think that's a great name. You'll never forget how she came into your life. You've got to promise me you'll help take good care of her, that you'll help to feed her and give her water. A kitten like this has to eat even more often than you do. Do you think you can be that responsible?"

"I can feed her."

"I'm sure your mom will help and show you at first. But then we'll see how much of a big boy you can be."

It was obvious to Jazzy that Brooks would make a wonderful father. When he looked up, their gazes met, and she wondered if he guessed what she was thinking. They'd never talked about children because they never expected their marriage to be a real one. She wanted children, but she wanted to do it right.

Brooks was helping the kitty back into her box. "I'll take her out to the desk for you. Jazzy will give you an itemized bill."

"My husband would have had a fit if he had seen what this was going to cost. But I figure, I'll just use the money he would have spent on beer this month."

Jazzy typed a few things into the computer and printed out the bill. Maggie wrote a check and handed it over.

Just as Timmy and his mom were leaving, Paige Dalton came into the office, surprising Jazzy. Paige was a fifth-grade teacher who was holding classes in her home. But she couldn't be holding classes if she was out and about. Jazzy had seen her over at the school several times and had liked her, though she really didn't know too much about her.

"Paige, it's good to see you. What brings you here? Do you have a small animal in your purse?"

Paige laughed and pushed her dark brown hair away from her cheek. "No, I don't. Not this time, anyway. I have a question for Brooks."

Brooks was watching mother and son leave, and Jazzy wished she could read his mind. Was he wondering what it would be like to be a father someday? Did he want to be a dad?

At the sound of his name, he turned toward Paige. "Hi, Paige. How can I help you?"

"The children have off today to work on special projects at their own homes. We're doing holiday customs around the world. Some of them are making baked goods. Some of the guys are building structures like the Eiffel Tower. Some of them are writing reports or recipes. Anyway, I gave them the day to work on them at home. And tomorrow is their presentation to the rest of the class. It should be fun. I'm taking our curriculum as is and trying to make it suit to what's happened around here. Teaching from my home is different from being in a classroom. Actually, they seem to be learning well in a relaxed atmosphere, but they do miss the socialization with their friends."

"I imagine they would," Jazzy said.

"So what do you need?" Brooks asked.

"Would you come talk to the class about being a veterinarian? I'm sure they'd love to hear. We're trying to do a different career each week, and I want to broaden their outlooks." She took a step closer to him. "I understand how busy you are, helping out with your dad's practice as well as this one. I'd only need about an hour of your time, and I think it would mean a lot to the children."

"I can't say no to the children now, can I?" Brooks asked with a smile. "Sure, I can spare an hour. What day next week would be good for you?"

"How about next Friday? Late morning…around eleven?"

"Jazzy will pencil it in." He motioned to the exam room. "I'm going to clean up in there."

Paige and Jazzy were left alone in the reception area. As Brooks disappeared, Paige put her hand over her mouth. "Oh, my gosh, I didn't even congratulate the two of you on your wedding. Best wishes!"

Jazzy didn't know what to say, so she just said, "Thank you."

"You got married really fast. It must have been a whirlwind romance."

Jazzy wasn't a mind reader, but she could see Paige seemed a little wistful. Was it because she wanted a whirlwind romance of her own? Or because her own heart had been broken?

Jazzy just hoped this marriage of convenience wouldn't break *her* heart.

* * *

The following evening, Jazzy made supper—soup again, so she could take some to Barrett—wondering how she could break the tension between her and Brooks. Clamping the lid on the soup, she turned it down to simmer, hoping Brooks wouldn't be too late.

As soon as she thought it, the garage door opened. She realized she was nervous and anxious as he came from the garage into the kitchen and strode into the mudroom.

She called a "hello" but he must not have heard her over the water running because he didn't call back. When he appeared in the kitchen, he'd discarded his jacket. There wasn't a welcoming expression on his face. He looked so serious, she was afraid of what might come out of his mouth next.

However, all he said was, "Do I have time to take a shower before dinner?"

"Sure. The soup can keep. The longer it cooks, the better it tastes."

Usually he bantered back. But after their argument last night, he obviously wasn't bantering. Had that been their first fight? Was he going to forgive her for not telling him about Griff, or for the things she'd said about what they were doing concerning his dad?

Chopping vegetables for a salad, she heard the shower running. She imagined him standing naked under that shower. She imagined tan lines from his working outdoors, let alone the muscles that would ripple when he moved. She imagined his wet hair, brown and slick, his smile as he beckoned her into the shower with him...

Abruptly, she cut off the fantasies. From what was

going on between them right now, that kind of envisioning belonged on another planet.

She'd finished making the salad and was slicing a loaf of crusty bread that she'd picked up at the bakery when she realized the shower had gone off a long while before. Was Brooks staying in his room to avoid her? Maybe he was making phone calls.

Leaving the kitchen, she walked down the hall to his bedroom. His door was partially open, and when she peeked inside, she saw him standing at the window, sweatpants riding low on his hips as he stared out into the black night. Something was off. Something was wrong.

She simply couldn't stay away. She had to know what was going on in his head. He didn't seem to hear the door when it creaked open because he didn't turn toward her.

"Brooks?" she called softly.

He still didn't turn toward her.

Crossing to the window, she touched his arm. "Is something wrong?"

His face still had the strained expression she'd seen when he walked in. His eyes bore a look of turmoil as he finally turned to look at her. "I'm a veterinarian and I'm supposed to stay detached from the animals I treat."

She had a bad feeling and dreaded what was coming. "It's hard to stay detached."

"I'm usually good at compartmentalizing—keeping the business of being a veterinarian on one side, patient care on the other side, personal life underneath it all. But today— I lost a foal. It was stillborn. Nothing I could do."

Looking away from her again, she knew he didn't want her to see the emotion he was feeling.

"I'm sorry, Brooks." She really could think of nothing else to say. No words helped in a situation like this.

He must have heard the heartfelt understanding in her words. He must have seen the longing in her eyes…her desire for everything between them to be right again. His voice was deeply husky as he said, "Jazzy."

Impulse led her to wrap her arms around him in a hug, to lift her face to his. Impulse must have gotten to him, too…because he bent his head and kissed her.

This wasn't a light, feathery kiss. This time, Brooks's mouth on hers was decidedly masterful, absolutely possessive, totally consuming. His tongue breached her lips in a way that said he needed—wanted—this kiss as much as she did.

She didn't need to breathe. All she wanted to do was feel—feel Brooks's desire in the way his arms tightened around her, feel it in the way his tongue swept her mouth, feel it in the way his body hardened against hers. His skin was hot as her hands explored his bare back. His muscles were taut under her fingertips. He was strength and desire and gentleness…and she loved him. Oh, how she loved him.

She thought it over and over again though she didn't say it. Too much was happening at once. Had he forgiven her for not telling him about Griff? Were his feelings going deeper, too? Did he want exactly what she wanted tonight?

He certainly seemed to because as she stroked her hands down his back and around to his hips, as her thumbs fingered the drawstring on his sweatpants, he groaned and broke off the kiss. For a moment she thought he might want to part like he had the other night, but tonight he looked at her differently.

Tonight he shook his head as if he couldn't fight desire anymore. Tonight he said, "I want you, Jazzy. Do you want me, too?"

No words of love there. Yet she heard deep emotion in his voice and saw it on his face. She was going to give in to it…give in to passion and hope for love.

"I want you." She put as much feeling into those three words as she could manage.

With a deep groan, he lifted her into his arms and she wrapped her legs around him. His fervent kisses distracted her so she didn't even realize he had carried her to the bed. As she sat on the edge of the bed, she clung to him, rubbing her nose into his neck, letting everything about him encompass her. His large hands slid under the hem of her sweater.

"You're going to have to let go of me if I'm going to get this off you."

She didn't want to let go of him, not ever.

He swiveled their bodies until he was sitting beside her on the bed, too. Lifting her sweater over her head, he made quick work of her bra and stared at her as if she were a beautiful piece of artwork…or a fascinating sculpture…or a woman he cared about. Maybe even…loved.

"You can touch me," she said softly, so wanting to hear what he felt about her.

He gave her a wry smile. "So can you."

They reached for each other at the same moment.

She untied the drawstring at his waist. He unsnapped her jeans.

In no time at all, they were naked on his big bed, facing each other, touching. Every stroke and every kiss meant so much because it had been taboo for so long. Ever since that first night when they'd flirted at the Ace in the Hole, they'd experienced the sexual electricity that had brought them to this moment.

When she laced her fingers in his hair, he caressed her thigh, his hand doing enticing things she could feel down deep inside. Her fingers played in his chest hair. After a speaking glance that said he was going to get serious now, he lowered his head to her breast. The tug of his lips on her nipple inspired sensations she'd never felt before. His tongue laving it made her call his name. His smile, filled with deep male satisfaction, led her to reach for him, enfold him in her hand, and feel the pulsing of his blood. He let out a long breath that told her she affected him just as he affected her.

But apparently he'd had enough of the foreplay. Sliding his palm to the apex of her thighs, he knew she had, too.

"Don't move," he rasped, as he reached for the nightstand and pulled out the drawer.

She kept her eyes closed, her breaths coming in short, shallow pants because each kiss and touch had readied her for what came next. She heard the rustle of foil, the packet tearing. A moment later, he was back with her, kissing her lips until she clung to him like a vine.

He rolled her onto her back and rose above her, but he didn't move to enter her. Gazing at her, he said, "I was jealous of that man you dated, and I took it out on you. I shouldn't have. You're the most honest woman I know."

It was an apology, and she knew saying he was jealous was hard for Brooks. There was no reason to dwell on it, or their argument. She reached for him and when he entered her, she felt wonderfully whole. She arched up to Brooks, wrapped her legs around him, and took him deeper. His groan of satisfaction made her feel proud, made her feel driven to give him everything she was and everything she could be. Each of his thrusts took her to a new plane of sensation. The melding of their bodies created a swirl of emotion she couldn't begin to grasp.

When they'd stood at the falls a couple of weeks ago, she'd felt awe near to this. But not anything this wide and deep and high. Not something as cataclysmically earth-shattering. This was *love*. It was so totally consuming that she didn't know if she'd ever be herself again.

As she held on to Brooks, light shattered, feelings washed over her, her body trembled and then shook with a climax so overwhelming, tears came to her eyes. Brooks's release came immediately after, and as they gasped for breath together and held on to each other, she knew their lives would never be the same.

The first sign that something was wrong was the way Brooks rolled away from her, with his eyes closed, and without a smile. The second was his terse "I'll be right back," as if they had something important to settle.

Jazzy's head was still spinning from making love

with him, and she hoped she was wrong about the feeling of doom that was stirring in her heart. Moments before, it had been filled with hope.

When Brooks returned from the bathroom, he didn't slide into bed with her, but rather sat on the edge. "That was a huge mistake."

She didn't know what she had expected to hear, but that wasn't it.

She was about to tell him she didn't regret anything about making love, when he said, "I think we should split up. We'll tell my dad it didn't work out. I'll still give you my grandmother's land, though."

Stunned, she couldn't begin to make sense of his words, let alone respond to them.

He went on, laying out his case. "Even if we tried to make a real marriage of this, I can't give you the marriage you deserve. With my own practice, watching over Dad's, I won't have time to sleep, let alone nurture a relationship. My mom had to cover for my dad more times than I can count. Whenever I had a school function, or sports event, she didn't complain, but he wasn't around. He was always working. When she got sick, my grandmother was there more than he was."

"Are you saying that I'm so different from your mom?"

"Oh, you're different all right, Jazzy. You say what you think. Even if she resented the time Dad worked, she never said. You couldn't be like that."

"How do you know I'd resent it?"

"I just know."

To her dismay, she realized he was thinking of

Lynnette again. He might not be comparing her to his mother, but he was comparing her to another woman who'd let him down. And that just made her angry.

"This isn't about your mom *or* your dad working too much. It's about *your* broken engagement. It's about a woman being unfaithful to you and walking out."

His silence told her she'd hit the mark. Still, he concluded, "No matter what it's about, we'd end up hating each other. I don't want that. Do you?"

Reaching for the sheet, she pulled it up, feeling the need to cover her body where she hadn't such a short time ago. But now everything was different. Brooks had succumbed to desire in a moment of weakness. He didn't love her. He couldn't, not if he wanted to end their marriage.

To top it all off, he began dressing quickly. And then he pulled his duffel bag from the closet.

"What are you doing?"

"I'm going to give Dallas a call and go bunk with him and his kids. I'm sure he won't mind, and he won't ask any questions."

"That's all you're concerned about, questions?" Brooks was building a new wall around himself, and Jazzy knew there wasn't anything she could say to knock it down. She'd found the man of her dreams and he didn't want her. He didn't need her.

All she could think of to say was, "Your father's going to be so upset."

Brooks gave her a long, hard look. "Not any more upset than he would be at the end of the year. This was a crazy idea. We were both foolish for thinking it could work."

With his boots on now, jeans and sweatshirts in his duffel, he was ready to go.

"I'm not going to stay here, Brooks. It's *your* place, not mine."

"Stay as long as you need to. This is *my* fault, not yours, Jazzy. I'll see a lawyer and get that land transferred over. I'll keep my word."

Then as if he couldn't stand to look at her another moment longer, he left.

Chapter Thirteen

Jazzy absolutely didn't know what to do. She'd cried most of the night. This morning she was trying to look at her options. But her feelings kept getting in the way. Should she go back to Thunder Canyon? Should she leave Brooks forever? She really couldn't think about that in spite of what he'd said.

Yet she knew she couldn't stay here in his condo. She couldn't walk into his bedroom and remember what they'd done…how she'd felt…how he'd claimed her. It would be impossible to stay here without envisioning the future she'd hoped they'd be able to share.

Tears threatened again. She swiped them away, knowing this was her own fault for risking her heart. Maybe she should have married Griff who was safe. But, no. She hadn't wanted safe and she still didn't. She wanted Brooks. But if he didn't want her, what could she do?

Picking up her cell phone, she dialed the number for Strickland's Boarding House. Fortunately, Melba answered. She certainly hadn't wanted to leave a message. "Melba, it's Jazzy Cates."

"Hi, honey. How are you? Getting used to married life?"

So what could she say to that? She could hang up and think of something else. She could drive herself back to Thunder Canyon.

Not yet.

"Melba, I need to know if you still have the room I was renting."

Silence met her question.

"You want your room back?"

"Is it still available?"

"Yes, it is. Did you and your young man have a fight?"

If it had been a fight, they could make up. If it had been a fight, maybe she would have gotten out all of her feelings. If it had been a fight, there could still be hope.

"You could say that. I just need to be by myself for a while."

"Well, come on back, honey. You know that coffee is always brewing and there's hot water for tea. I baked apple bread, too. Comfort food."

"Thanks, Melba. I'll be over soon."

After Jazzy packed her suitcase, after she got into her car and switched on the ignition, she backed out of Brooks's driveway. Instead of heading for town and Strickland's, she headed for the Bar S. She didn't expect Brooks to be at his dad's clinic this early. In fact, she didn't want to see him. She couldn't see him. Not until she felt as if she had her emotions all under control. But she *did* want to see his father. She had something to say to him and she just hoped he was in a receptive mood.

Barrett had a mug in his hand when he opened the door. "It's tea," he said with a broad smile. "Herbal. I've still cut caffeine out of my diet."

"Good for you," she said with as much enthusiasm as she could muster. She knew Barrett missed his coffee as much as he missed donuts. She'd brought him soup because she and Brooks hadn't eaten any last night, and she knew his dad liked it. Besides, it was a good excuse for stopping by.

She had two containers in the bag, and she said to him, "I brought you soup, enough to eat and freeze. Do you have a few minutes?"

"Sure. That teenager Brooks hornswoggled into helping me with chores won't get here for about an hour. He's catching on, but I still have to supervise."

Jazzy went inside the house to the kitchen. She stowed a container of soup in the refrigerator and the other one in the freezer. Barrett's freezer was still fairly stacked with other dinners she had made for him. Maybe they'd be the last. Maybe she wouldn't be seeing Barrett again. That thought deeply saddened her.

"Okay, missy. Sit down and tell me what's going on. You don't have the usual spring in your step. What did my son do now?"

For some reason, Barrett's comment made Jazzy angry. "You've got to stop blaming Brooks for trying to do the right thing."

Barrett looked a little surprised at her explosion. "You *do* need to sit down. You need some of this herbal tea more than I do." He pulled out a chair for her and pointed to it.

As she sat she said, "Brooks didn't do anything wrong. He tried to do something right."

Barrett sat across from her and hiked up one brow. "And—"

"He's the most honest, value-oriented man I know. The only thing he did was try to…try to protect *you*."

After a long pause, Barrett's voice was wary as he encouraged, "Go on."

She was going to get it all out. Every bit of it. There was simply no reason why she shouldn't. Simply no reason why Barrett shouldn't know all of the truth. "If you had just trusted Brooks enough to hand down the practice to him…if you had been reasonable about your own health, then I never would have gotten caught up in a pretend marriage that turned out to be not so pretend!"

Barrett leaned back in his chair and eyed her. "Let's slow down a bit so I can make sure I understand what you're saying. You think I should have handed the practice down to Brooks?"

"Of course you should have. Or at least formed a joint venture after he graduated. It wasn't his fault Lynnette took up with another guy. She didn't have what it takes to be a veterinarian's wife. She didn't have what it takes to live in a small town. You blamed him for that."

"Is that what he said?"

"Of course that's *not* what he said. He blamed himself, too. And that was reinforced by *you* blaming him."

"I never knew why they broke up," Barrett muttered. "He didn't tell me. He just said something about long hours and her not wanting to live in a small town."

"That was only part of it. And she blamed the breakup on that. But she hurt him badly, Mr. Smith, and that's why he hasn't wanted to get involved with anyone since."

"Until you came along."

She sighed, took a deep breath and plunged in. "The night I officially met Brooks, he'd argued with you about your health. He was so frustrated and so worried. That's why he decided to set up a private practice. I happened to be on the bar stool next to him. We'd run into each other before that, but not officially introduced. That night, we talked. He asked me to come work for him."

"Must have liked you right away to do that."

"Maybe so. I don't know. But the icing on our wedding cake was because you wouldn't listen to reason when you were in the hospital. That day, Brooks asked me to marry him. We made a deal. He offered me his grandmother's land if I married him for a year. He figured in a year, he could help get your health turned around and then everything would go back to normal."

She shook her head. "There is no normal. Last night, he realized…he realized it's not going to work. He wants to split up. He doesn't want to be married."

Barrett cocked his head, studied her carefully and she suspected he could see way too much. He cleared his throat. "I can see the Smith pride has gotten us both into a peck of trouble. I *do* trust Brooks. But the truth is—I could see him going down the same road I took. I'd been a true workaholic all my life. I saw my family suffer because of it. I knew only one thing could save Brooks—if he found a woman he cared about as much as he cared about himself…as much as he cared about his furry patients. I wanted him to find that woman and build a life with her. I wanted him to marry and settle down so he'd have a reason to come home."

Jazzy's dejection must have shown on her face.

"He said the marriage isn't going to work out, huh? Do you believe that?"

When Jazzy didn't respond, Barrett leaned across the table and patted her hand with his. "Do you love him?"

She couldn't keep the tears from her voice. "I do."

"You know what? I think he loves you, too, whether he admits it or not. I've seen the way he looks at you. And you can't tell me he would have gotten himself tied up to a woman if he didn't care for her. I don't know what happened between the two of you, but give him a little time and maybe he'll come to his senses."

"What if he doesn't?"

Barrett's heavy brow hiked up. "Then he's a danged fool."

Brooks finished with his last patient of the morning at Buckskin Clinic, checked out Mr. Gibbs with his Doberman pinscher, handled the man's check and watched him leave. Then he glanced around the empty reception area, heard no sounds of Jazzy moving around in the exam rooms and realized how much he missed her. He not only missed her by his side here in the office… he missed her, period. Had she driven back to Thunder Canyon? Or was she still at his place?

His place. He had begun thinking of it as *their* place. Everything—every memory, every touch and kiss—that they'd experienced last night came back to haunt him. Thinking about it all was like a punch in the gut. He thought about staying with Dallas and his kids again tonight. The boys had been a distraction, that was for sure. But even Dallas's kids couldn't distract him from the memory of the look in Jazzy's eyes when he'd said he wanted out…when he'd said their deal was no longer a deal…when he'd said his father might as well know sooner rather than later.

His dad.

Brooks had to settle everything with him now. He didn't want his father finding out about the breakup of his marriage from somebody else.

Fifteen minutes later, Brooks was in his father's kitchen, watching his dad ladle soup from a plastic container into a bowl. "You look as if you need some lunch," Barrett said. "What's up?"

Brooks didn't know where to begin. "Jazzy and I… we—"

Barrett pushed the soup into the microwave, shut the door and set the timer. "You and Jazzy what?"

"We don't…we didn't have a real marriage. She's probably on her way back to Thunder Canyon."

With those words the rest of Brooks's sorry tale poured out—how they'd connected at the Ace in the Hole, how she'd agreed to work for him, how he'd come up with the brilliant idea of a marriage of convenience. "I made an appointment to see a lawyer this week and transfer Grandma's land to her." He expected a blowup from his father at that, but he didn't get it.

"Are you sure you want to do that?" was all his father asked.

"Jazzy deserves it for putting up with this whole situation. For—"

"*Why* does Jazzy deserve it? She went into this thing with open eyes just like you did. Fools, both of you. But consenting fools."

"Look, Dad, we just never realized what was going to happen. We thought we could keep it a business agreement and we couldn't."

"So feelings got involved?" his father asked.

"Hell, yes, feelings got involved," Brooks erupted, standing up, walking around the table. "And there's not a thing I can do about them. I'm not marriage material. Working the two practices is going to keep me swamped up to my eyeballs. Besides, there's a reason Lynnette broke our engagement. There's a reason she fell for someone else. She said it was the hours, but it was something deeper than that. I was missing something—something as a man—that would keep her there."

Had this been the real reason he hadn't dated for the past four years? Was this the real reason he kept himself guarded where women were concerned? He was clearly lacking some special ingredient he needed to be a good husband and maybe a father someday.

"Brooks," his father said sharply.

He stopped pacing and stared at his dad.

"You're missing *nothing*. Did it ever occur to you that your relationship with Lynnette was missing something? Maybe *she* was missing a loyalty factor that led to her infidelity."

Brooks's mouth dropped open.

"Jazzy was here earlier. She explained what the two of you did. She gave me a dressing-down because I didn't trust you enough to hand over my practice. She told me about Lynnette and added that my lack of faith in you didn't help the situation. I've got to tell you, son. I *do* have faith in you. I *am* proud of you. But I wanted you to find a woman like your mom who could ground you. I wanted you with a woman who could make a home for you. I wanted you to have a wife to be the center of your world…who could keep you from working too long and too much. I should have made your mom the center of my world and I didn't. If I had, maybe she wouldn't have died so soon. If I had, maybe I would have seen the symptoms. *I* would have, should have been taking care of her at the end, not your grandmother. I did everything all wrong, and I didn't want you doing it wrong, too."

Brooks had never known any of this. But that's because he and his dad had never really talked. Not about the kind of things that mattered. Stunned, he asked, "So you blame yourself for Mom's death?"

"I blame myself for not loving her the right way. I blame myself for being pigheaded, in denial and too focused on work that served like a shield so I didn't have to give too much of myself. Don't you make the same damn mistake."

The microwave beeped. Barrett removed the soup bowl and put it on the table. "So what happened between you and Jazzy that made this whole thing blow up?"

Oh, no. Brooks wasn't going there.

Barrett narrowed his eyes. "Fine. My guess is your marriage of convenience got a little inconvenient. You're both confused because things happened so fast."

"I'm not confused," Brooks said, realizing now he had been miserable since he'd left Jazzy in his condo.

"Do you want out of the marriage?" his father demanded to know.

Last night when he'd made love to Jazzy, he'd realized in a blinding flash of earth-shattering proportions that he *had* been making love to her. It wasn't just sex. It had been so much more that the experience had rattled and disconcerted and even panicked him. He'd given her his word their marriage would be a business deal. He'd gone back on his word, which was something he *never* did.

"Not confused, huh?" his father asked with a sly smile. "Seems to me you're *plenty* confused. So think about a few things. How would you feel if Jazzy left for Thunder Canyon and never came back? How would you feel if you didn't see her every day? Just how would you feel if Jazzy Cates Smith got involved with someone else?"

Brooks didn't know where to turn. Facing those questions made him want to ram his fist through a wall. And why was that?

The fact was that the sexual electricity between him and Jazzy had wired him since he'd met her. But even more than that, her sweetness and caring, her perky outlook, lifted him up above a place where he'd been. She'd become the sunlight in his days, the moonlight in his nights. She'd become someone he treasured, a woman he respected...and *loved*. Jazzy had become the epitome of everything he'd been running from and everything he'd hoped for.

She was everything he wanted.

"So," Barrett drawled. "If you're not confused, just what do you feel for her?"

Brooks sighed. "I love her."

"Then why are you sitting here eating lunch with me? Go get her."

"I don't know where she is. She might have driven back to Thunder Canyon."

"She didn't. Not yet. She's at Strickland's."

Brooks started for the door.

Barrett called after him, "For what it's worth, she's in love with you, too. She has to be to put up with me."

Brooks prayed his dad was right as he climbed into his truck and picked up his cell phone. He skimmed through his contacts and dialed Strickland's, hoping to get Melba. He did.

"Melba, its Brooks Smith. Is Jazzy there?"

"I just took her a cup of tea a little while ago. Do you want me to get her?"

"No. I just wanted to make sure she was there."

"She's pretty upset," Melba told him. "Are you going to upset her more?"

"I certainly hope not. Can you keep her there if she tries to go out? I should be there in about twenty minutes."

"She's not going anywhere. She doesn't want anyone to see her crying."

Brooks felt as low as he could possibly feel. The last thing he'd ever wanted to do was hurt Jazzy. So he told Melba, "I'll see what I can do about that."

Twenty minutes later to the minute, he stood in front of Jazzy's door, a bouquet of roses in his hand. Thank goodness Nina had had some fresh flowers. Maybe they'd at least get him in to talk to Jazzy. He knocked.

Jazzy called through the door, "I'm okay, Melba. Really. I don't need any more tea."

"It's not Melba," he called back.

When Jazzy opened her door, slowly, as if she was afraid to let him in, he could easily see she was miserable, too. He held out the roses to her, taking in everything about the woman he loved, trying to absorb the fact that she held his future happiness in her hands.

"I know these will never be enough to make up for all the mistakes I made. But I want you to come home with me."

Jazzy's expression changed from cautious to defiant. "I did that before and you left."

"That's because I was a fool."

She didn't take the roses, and she crossed her arms over her chest. "You're not a fool anymore? What's changed?"

He deserved that. He deserved her not making this easy. He stepped inside her room, closed the door and laid the roses on the bed. Then he faced her, knowing this couldn't be done in half measure. "I didn't ask you to marry me on a whim."

Jazzy's arms uncrossed as she dropped them to her sides…and she waited.

Taking a risk, he took her hands in his and pulled her closer. "I might not have realized it the exact moment I sat on that stool at the Ace in the Hole, but you're everything I should have been looking for, everything I missed, everything I want. I love you, Jazzy. I don't know when it happened and I don't know why. Maybe it was when you first smiled at me. Maybe it was when you painted my office. Maybe it was when we went to the Falls. I know now it was before I said 'I do.' Making love with you was absolutely incredible. But I felt overwhelmed with desires I didn't even understand. But now I do."

Since she wasn't pulling away, since she seemed to be listening, since her eyes were glistening with unshed tears, he pulled her arms up around his neck and held her in a loving embrace. "I want a real marriage with you, Jazzy. I want to build a life, a future, a home with you. Can you forgive how stupid I've been and be my wife through thick and thin, better and worse, today and forever?"

"Oh, Brooks..."

When she said his name like that all he wanted to do was love her forever—

His heated kiss exposed his longing, his desire, the love he felt and the love he hoped to feel in the future.

She broke off the kiss, cupped his face in her hands, and said, "I love you, too, Brooks. I want to stand beside you, work beside you, fall asleep in your arms every night and have your babies."

"Babies?" he asked with a quirked brow.

"Babies," she assured him.

Sweeping her into his arms, he laughed and carried her to the single bed. When he kissed her again, he didn't stop and neither did she. They'd found their future in each other's arms.

Epilogue

Jazzy and Brooks walked through the field, holding gloved hands. The weather had turned colder, but they didn't care about the chill. This was something they wanted to do. They glanced at each other often, then studied their surroundings.

When they stopped in the midst of field grass about two hundred yards from the road, Jazzy said, "I can tell Mom and Dad are accepting our marriage now. They want to know how they can help with plans for the house."

"Our visit with them over the weekend brought us closer. When your dad and I went riding, he was almost friendly!"

"They could see we're in love."

Brooks grinned at her. "Because we didn't leave our bedroom till late Saturday morning?"

"Maybe," Jazzy said with a laugh. "Or maybe it's because when we look at each other, anyone within fifty feet can tell. We give off signals like Laila and Jackson, Abby and Cade, Annabel and Thomas do."

"Give me a signal," Brooks said, teasing her and bringing her close for a kiss. Their passion caught fire until Brooks broke away and raggedly stated, "If we don't want to make love in the middle of a field in freezing weather, we'd better concentrate on why we came." He waved to the east. "I can see the house sitting on that rise. Do you want one story or two?"

"I like those plans you found for a two-story log home. And I was thinking…"

"Uh-oh. Always dangerous."

She swatted his arm.

He hugged her, amusement dancing in his eyes. "Just teasing. What were you thinking?"

"I could start taking business courses online so I know how to run the operational side of a horse-rescue ranch. What do you think?"

"I think that's a terrific idea. Self-serving on my part because I want as much time with you as we can manage. To that end, I'm interviewing two possible partners this week. One is driving all the way from Bozeman. I'm video conferencing with the other. Dad's going to sit in."

Suddenly they heard a truck rumbling down the access road. "Speak of the devil," Brooks said in an amused tone.

Barrett climbed from his truck and leisurely walked toward them. "I thought I'd give you two a little time out here then come put in my two cents before you go back to Kalispell. Which, by the way, seems like a commute you don't need."

"Nothing in Rust Creek Falls is available, Dad. I spoke with the real-estate agent again this morning."

"Actually, something *is* available," his father assured him.

"Just what do you know that we don't?" Brooks kept his arm around Jazzy's waist.

"I was thinking," his father said.

"It's going around," Jazzy joked with a glance at Brooks.

Barrett ignored her comment and went on, looking a little…nervous? "It will take at least six months for you to get a place built. Especially if we have a rough winter. In fact, you might have to wait until spring to start construction."

"That's possible," Brooks conceded.

"So why don't you come stay with me?" Barrett hurriedly continued. "You can have the whole upstairs and as much privacy as you want. You can even make a spare bedroom into your own sitting room with a TV. After work, you can go your way and I can go mine. What do you think?"

Jazzy was totally surprised by the offer and Brooks seemed to be, too.

Brooks said, "I can't give you a decision right now. Jazzy and I will have to talk about it."

"Talking is a good thing when you're married. I'll let you to it. But don't stay out here too long or you'll freeze your tails off."

As quickly as Barrett had appeared, he gunned the engine of his truck and drove away in a spit of gravel.

Brooks squeezed Jazzy nearer to combine their warmth. "We could go sit in the truck."

"You think this is going to be a long discussion?" she asked, studying his face.

"I don't know. Is it? Tell me what you honestly think. Shouldn't newlyweds have total privacy?"

"That depends. It seems to me if we want privacy, we can find it—in the barn, in the clinic at the end of the day, in an upstairs hideaway. I really think your dad means what he says. We could have our own place up there. And...we wouldn't have to worry about him."

"It would be temporary...just until we get the house built."

"Exactly. Who knows? Till then maybe we can convince him to date."

"You are *such* an optimist."

"Isn't that why you married me?"

He shook his head. "I married you because I was falling hopelessly in love with you."

"And I with you."

As snowflakes began a fluttering shower around them, they kissed again with a fire that could warm any cold winter day...a fire that could last a lifetime.

* * * * *

Warm up for the holidays with
A MAVERICK UNDER THE MISTLETOE
by Brenda Harlen,
the next installment in the new
Special Edition continuity
MONTANA MAVERICKS:
RUST CREEK COWBOYS
On sale November 2013,
wherever Harlequin books are sold.

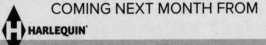
Available October 22, 2013

#2293 A MAVERICK UNDER THE MISTLETOE
Montana Mavericks: Rust Creek Cowboys
by Brenda Harlen
When Sutter Traub had a falling-out with his family, he took off to Seattle. But now he's back—and so is Paige Dutton, the woman he left behind. Can Sutter and Paige mend their broken hearts together?

#2294 HOW TO MARRY A PRINCESS
The Bravo Royales • by Christine Rimmer
Tycoon Noah Cordell has a thing for princesses—specifically, Alice Bravo-Calabretti. Noah is a man who knows what he wants, but can he finagle his way into this free-spirited beauty's heart?

#2295 THANKSGIVING DADDY
Conard County: The Next Generation • by Rachel Lee
Pilot Edie Clapton saves navy SEAL Seth Hardin's life—and they celebrate with a passionate encounter. Little does Edie know she has a bundle of joy on the way...and possibly the love of a lifetime.

#2296 HOLIDAY BY DESIGN
The Hunt for Cinderella • by Patricia Kay
Fashion designer Joanna Spinelli has nothing in common with straitlaced Marcus Barlow—until they go into business together. Can impetuous Joanna and inflexible Marcus meet in the middle—where passion might ignite?

#2297 THE BABY MADE AT CHRISTMAS
The Cherry Sisters • by Lilian Darcy
Lee Cherry is living the life in Aspen, Colorado. But when she finds herself pregnant from a fling with handsome Mac Wheeler, she panics. Mac follows her home, but little do they know what Love plans for them both....

#2298 THE NANNY'S CHRISTMAS WISH
by Ami Weaver
Maggie Thelan wants to find her long-lost nephew, while Josh Tanner is eager to raise his son in peace. When Maggie signs on, incognito, as Cody's nanny, no one expects sparks to fly, but a true family begins to form....

HSECNM1013

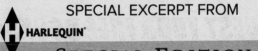
Sutter Traub is a heartbreaker...something Paige Dalton knows only too well. Which is why she's determined to stay as far as she can from her ex! But Rust Creek's prodigal son has come home to help his brother win an election—and to win back the heart of the woman he's never been able to forget...

***

"Sutter?"

He yanked his gaze from her chest. "Yeah?"

She huffed out a breath and drew the lapels closer together. Despite her apparent indignation, the flush in her cheeks and the darkening of those chocolate-colored eyes proved that she was feeling the same awareness that was heating his blood.

"I said there's beer and soda in the fridge, if you want a drink while you're waiting."

"Sorry, I wasn't paying attention," he admitted. "I was thinking about how incredibly beautiful and desirable you are."

She pushed her sodden bangs away from her face. "I'm a complete mess."

"Do you remember when we cut through the woods on the way home from that party at Brooks Smith's house and you slipped on the log bridge?"

She shuddered at the memory. "It wouldn't have been a big deal if I'd fallen into water, but the recent drought had reduced the stream to a trickle, and I ended up covered in muck and leaves."

And when they'd gotten back to the ranch, they'd stripped out of their muddy clothes and washed one another under the warm spray of the shower. Of course, the scrubbing away of dirt had soon turned into something else, and they'd made love until the water turned cold.

"Even then—covered in mud from head to toe—you were beautiful."

"You only said that because you wanted to get me naked."

"Just because I wanted to get you naked doesn't mean it wasn't true. And speaking of naked…"

"I should put some clothes on," Paige said.

"Don't go to any trouble on my account."

***

*We hope you enjoyed this sneak peek
from award-winning author Brenda Harlen's
new Harlequin® Special Edition book,
A MAVERICK UNDER THE MISTLETOE,
the next installment in*
MONTANA MAVERICKS: RUST CREEK COWBOYS.
Available next month.

HSEEXP1013